SAS
WORLD WAR TWO
BABCOCK'S REVENGE

WHISKEY-JACK PETERS

BOOK 2 - INTO GERMANY

SAS
WORLD WAR TWO
BABCOCK'S REVENGE
BOOK 2
All rights reserved.
Copyright © 2021 by Mr. F. McLeod (C.S.N. V7662792)
ISBN: 978-0-6451026-7-3
No part of this book may be reproduced or transmitted in any form or by any means, electronic or mechanical, including photocopying, recording, or by any information storage and retrieval system, without permission in writing from the author. Contact us at teslabookstore@vivaldi.net.
First Edition published 2021

SAS
WORLD WAR TWO

BABCOCK'S REVENGE

WHISKEY-JACK PETERS

BOOK 2 - INTO GERMANY

Table Of Contents

Acknowledgements...5
Prologue..6
Chapter 1..35
Chapter 2..50
Chapter 3..61
Chapter 4..73
Chapter 5..83
Chapter 6..99
Chapter 7..109
Chapter 8..122
Chapter 9..134
Chapter 10..141
Chapter 11..149
Chapter 12..165

Acknowledgements

As I continue to write more stories in this series, I have been blessed to have the help of many talented people along the way. My cover designer, Giusy D'anna, who lives in Italy, did fantastic work for me once again. Then, a fine man from Argentina named Darío de los Santos did all of the file conversions to paperback and e-books for me and got them to all work properly. My editor, Maxwell Anderson, was also a tremendous help—working out of Japan.

Additionally, I have been very lucky to receive some very helpful life lessons from Richard Hungerford, who served his country in the Special Air Service and who is now an instructor at the Warrior's Path Academy in Australia. You'll see many of his teachings within this story.

I thank you all for your contributions!

Prologue

November 15, 1942

On the deck of the British Submarine known as the *HMS Trident*, twenty-seven-year-old Corporal Randy O'Brien made last-minute inspections of his collapsible folboat before he gave the signal to his helper that he was ready to depart on his mission. He made damn sure his weapon was inside the boat—and that it was secure. Once he confirmed it was in place, he looked around for his paddle and saw that it was still where he had left it. He took several deep breaths as he looked out at the caps that were breaking on the waves in the darkness of the night.

"I'm ready. Thumbs up," the corporal said out loud as he checked his personal flotation device that was fastened to his upper torso. However, the submarine crew on the deck couldn't hear him with the wind howling as it was. O'Brien gave a thumbs up, which prompted the petty officer, who had been helping him, to stand up and wave towards the con tower with a flashlight that had a red lens attached to it. He waved in the commander's direction, hoping that he would see the signal.

The commander had been watching in silence and saw the red light moving in the darkness to catch his attention. Once he saw it, he looked down into the open hatch. "Prepare to dive," Commander Flint ordered.

His second in command, who was just going down through the con tower hatch, repeated the order so all could hear it below him. "Prepare to dive! Man your stations, people."

Back on the deck, one of the crew held onto the folboat while O'Brien stood up and got into his collapsible boat. "You're sure you got everything, Corporal?" Petty Officer Mills asked as the Australian commando positioned himself, with the folboat still resting on the front deck of the British sub. His eyes were met with a confirming nod. "I'm ready . . . although I can't even see the bloody island, mate!"

The petty officer looked off into the darkness and pointed in the direction the Coastwatcher needed to travel. "The island's that way, and it's going to be one hell of a trip to get there. Good luck, Corporal!"

O'Brien nodded with appreciation in his eyes. "Thanks for your help getting things ready, mate. This is going to be epic!"

Petty Officer Mills nodded his head. "No problem. Good luck, Corporal. Anything else you want to say or ask me before we head back inside?"

The corporal shook his head and smiled back at him and the able seaman, who had been holding his folboat steady. Then, he watched them both head back to the front hatch that they'd all come out of. After they climbed down and shut the hatch, he realized he was now on his own in the great Pacific Ocean.

A minute later, the submarine began to dive, leaving Corporal O'Brien out on the open sea by himself in the cold rainy darkness as the waves pounded his small boat relentlessly. It wasn't an easy mission, but he'd volunteered for it. O'Brien was only a few months out of the training cycle for the Australian commando forces, and when they asked for volunteers for this mission, he'd presented himself for consideration.

As he climbed over each wave, he soon discovered there were others that would hit him from the side, almost turning his boat over at the same time. If he allowed that to happen, he wouldn't likely get it back right-side up. It was a hell of a storm to be in, and he considered it to be more of a graduation test than the actual course he'd been able to get through back in Australia. The most important piece of kit he had right now besides the folboat was his paddle. If he lost that, it was truly game over.

He'd been briefed about the storm earlier that evening and had thought he could still get to shore in an hour, but he was ten miles out at sea and the ocean was doing everything it could do to slow him down and prevent him from succeeding. The salt-water spray soaked his face, and he felt cold. Bitterly cold. It was the winter solstice, so he had tried to prepare himself mentally for the challenge, but now it was a mental game. He borrowed from his brother Vinnie's mental toughness because he played rugby at the national level and when it came time to play New Zealand or South Africa, there only was complete focus for every second of the game. That's what Vinnie had once told him. Otherwise, the opposing team would stomp all over you.

A win for the other side out here meant his own death, so he doubled down and paddled hard. He kept his brother in his thoughts and pretended they were together on the field working in unison at a rugby final against the All Blacks. It was do-or-die time, he reckoned. Luckily, the storm gave him good cover though. The waves were choppy, which made it dangerous travelling for any ship or small boat like his. If he made it to shore, the chances of being seen were minimal, which was a good thing for him.

It took some time, and a whole lot of energy was expended to keep himself right-side-up, but eventually, he saw a dark shape off in the distance. Slowly, its shape became more pronounced as he drew closer. There was also a reef that the waves crashed over, causing white illumination as water hit exposed rock.

He did his best not to tip over the boat as he raced over the reef atop some fast-moving waves. It felt as if he was almost ready to stand up on top of a surfboard as the water beneath him picked up speed, churning over the coral reef. O'Brien was soaked to the bone, and he was shivering. He felt a cramp starting to form in his right hamstring, but he persevered because he knew he wasn't far away from reaching his objective. Still, he was having a tough time trying to relax the tightening muscle group in his leg while maintaining equilibrium.

Twenty minutes later, the corporal paddled his boat onto the shore, but he didn't waste time mucking about. With all the strength he could muster while still under the cover of darkness, he pulled his boat out of the sea and dragged it towards shore. After a moment of looking around, using his peripheral vision in an attempt to spot enemy movement, he began to drag it up onto the beach. After looking around and listening for unnatural sounds, he decided he was safe for the moment, so he began to unpack his gear and get it all up to the treeline ahead of him.

After spending the first half-hour getting his kit hidden amongst the tree canopy and thick island vegetation, the next task was to collapse his boat and carry it up off the beach into the area where he'd put his gear. He knew he had to bury the boat so he could access it again, but his hiding spot couldn't be so close to the beach. He needed to be smart. O'Brien figured he needed to go inland for a few hundred yards, and hopefully, by then, he would find the right spot to bury it and camouflage the area so no one would be able to detect it.

The final things that he needed to take care of were the footprints and markings of the folboat that were still visible in the otherwise smoothed out beach sand. As he ventured back out onto the beach, he saw an albatross drifting around on the air currents just offshore. He watched it coast in the air with such grace. Its wings were massive, and he took a second to appreciate how it could survive out there in all forms of weather.

After the beach was cleaned up and the tracks were brushed away, the Australian went back into the vegetation and headed inland with his rucksack and rifle. He stopped after a few yards because it wasn't easygoing, as he suddenly realized that he might not find his kit again once he went back for the boat. The darkness wasn't making things easy for him, but this was the job he'd volunteered for, so he stopped, pulled out his compass, and focused on the survival breathing methods he had been taught. Combat breathing techniques helped to fill the brain with good levels of oxygen, thus mitigating stress.

After taking a bearing and pulling out his counting beads, he began walking deeper into the dense growth. It took him another forty-five minutes of moving through the jungle until he discovered an area where he thought it would be good to bury his boat. As quietly as he could, he took off his gear and hung it up on a broken branch so that no snakes or spiders could crawl into his rucksack and make a new home for themselves. He then put his weapon on a rock so no sand would get into it, and once those two things were taken care of, he started to clear the area so that when he came back with the boat, he'd recognize the spot again.

When the corporal reached the boat, he checked his watch and found that it was already two in the morning. He was staying warm with all the movements he was making, but he felt tired. Though he wanted to sleep for a bit, he wasn't ready for that yet. The corporal still had to deal with his folboat. As he looked it over, it seemed that everything was still in good working order. It didn't appear to have been ripped in the reef, and this put a smile on his face. At least he still had a boat that was seaworthy in case he needed to escape the island. That could surely mean life or death, depending on the circumstances.

It seemed awfully heavy, but he managed to get the load on his back where he could support the most weight, and then he checked his compass while being half bent forwards. Once he had his bearings, he set off and slowly made his way back to the burying site, which he knew would take a good while to reach under the cover of darkness and through such thick vegetation.

By four that morning, the young commando had finished hiding his foldable boat and wondered how much time he had until the sun rose. He had made his own hammock using cordage while in the submarine and was keen to try it out. He lifted his flashlight, which had a red lens on it, and looked for his rucksack. As he opened up the main compartment, he looked inside before attempting to grab what he was looking for.

After he rolled it out on the ground, he took one end of the hammock and tied it five feet up a tree trunk, and then when that was securely tied, he walked over to the other end and tied that to another tree at the same height as the first one. O'Brien then tested it by sitting in the middle, and thankfully, it held his weight.

"What a relief," he said to himself as he carefully got comfortable. Randy was all smiles as he went horizontal. For a few minutes he was happy, and then the raindrops started hitting his face. "Bloody hell!"

O'Brien realized that the clouds above the jungle canopy were about to let a ton of rain fall on him. There was a solution, though. He had a canvas tarp that he'd cut up for a make shift roof before he'd left his quarters, and now it was going to come in real handy, but it meant getting off of the hammock again, which he soon found out wasn't as easy as he'd imagined it being. As soon as he put one leg out and shifted his weight, the corporal fell flat on his face. He felt like an idiot, but he didn't stay on the jungle floor to think about it. He got up and dusted himself off.

Randy went into his rucksack once more and pulled out his rolled-up piece of canvas as the rain started coming down through the jungle canopy. He'd been smart and had invested some time while on the submarine, sewing in eyelets so he could attach some cordage to each corner of the canvas. That was going to be a lifesaver. Making haste, he moved to four different trees and positioned the tarp above his hammock as the rain came down harder and harder all around him.

By the time he had finished securing the lines and positioning it over his sleeping spot, the young Australian was soaked again but thankful to have a roof over his head as he carefully eased himself into the hammock once again and lay back down. For some time, all he could do was listen to the sound of the rain landing on the canvas and the vegetation surrounding him. It kept him up for some time until he relaxed enough to fall asleep.

Corporal O'Brien woke up in his hammock at around 6 a.m. when some gulls announced that they were starting their search for breakfast over on the beach. He hadn't slept for very long, but he was grateful for the two hours that he did get. Randy then extended his arms and grabbed the edges of his hammock as he carefully manoeuvred his body so he wouldn't fall out.

Daylight had broken, so Randy could now take in his surroundings. His rifle was fine because he'd kept it beside him while he had been sleeping, and his rucksack was still hanging from the branch where he'd placed it a few hours before. He stepped away from the hammock and then walked over to the tree where he'd hung his pack.

Fidgeting around in one of the outside pockets, he pulled out a fresh pair of socks and sat down on a rock as he took his boots off again and put a pair of clean socks on. As he did his laces up, he looked around but didn't see any signs of creepy crawlies or snakes that might be lurking about the leaf matter surrounding him.

The daylight could scarcely penetrate the jungle canopy, and he wondered just how bright things were out on the beach where he'd landed the previous night. He hoped that he'd done a good enough job covering up his tracks and that no enemy forces were on the island, but only time would tell if that were true or not.

Lost in thought, he walked over to an unsuspecting bush, undid his fly, and had a whiz. After Randy was done, he decided that he should look at where he had buried his boat and review the job he'd done.

After walking over to the spot, he could see that it needed more camouflage, so he gathered up some leaf litter and placed it around the area until it looked like no one had been there before. He carefully looked around to make sure there were no straight lines or any heel marks on the substrate, which might give his presence away. After a final inspection of the area, he was satisfied that he'd done a decent job of hiding his boat and decided to take a break.

As he took in some water from his canteen, O'Brien decided to go back to his camp area and take a look at that area too. When he got there, he looked at his canvas tarp, which had kept the water off of him quite well. His hammock underneath it had been successful as well, though hard to sleep in.

It had taken Corporal O'Brien a long time to get used to sleeping in a hammock. A person sleeping in one didn't get the luxury of rolling over onto their side, and if they tried, they usually ended up spilling out and lying on the ground pretty quickly. But this time around, Randy was so utterly exhausted that another two hours sounded just fine to him as he waited for more of the morning light to come and rescue him from the darkness of the island's vegetation—trees, elephant ear plants, and bamboo.

The rest of the day was spent patrolling around the initial spot where he'd buried his boat and set up his hammock. After completing multiple box searches around the area, Randy was confident that he knew the obstacles that were near his hideout. By sunset, O'Brien knew where to refill his water bottles because one thing he had to do was keep himself properly hydrated. It was late in the afternoon when he concluded that there were no Japanese soldiers within his vicinity.

At 4 p.m., O'Brien inspected his feet in front of his shelter. While he set up his washbasin, he thought about what he would do the next day. The young commando needed to push deeper into the jungle so he could get closer to his objective now that he'd acclimated himself to the local surroundings. While doing so he didn't want to be spotted by a Japanese foot patrol, but he believed he knew a way to travel that offered a low degree of risk. While he set the small metal basin on the ground, he remembered that the intelligence officer on the submarine hadn't been able to decisively say whether or not the island was occupied and controlled by the Japanese. He'd been told to assume so. That meant O'Brien needed to make tactical and strategic decisions before comfort at all times.

One of the unfortunate things he would have to deal with while staying on the island was the wet jungle heat. It was like being in a sauna that one couldn't escape from, and he was constantly sweating. His clothes were soaked by the end of the day, and they didn't seem to be dry by the next morning. Moving around in wet clothes all the time would wear down his skin integrity, so he made a mental note to himself to keep watching his skin under his arms, between his toes, and in his crotch. The best thing he could do was apply foot powder in all of those places to keep the moisture build-up from getting out of hand and causing skin rot. He'd had enough lectures to know how to prevent that from happening.

When darkness announced itself, Corporal O'Brien went back to his hammock and listened to the sounds of the island wildlife as he ate a meal of tinned meat and some biscuits. The birds were showing no signs of going off from their baseline of normal chatter before they settled in for the night, so that was a good sign to him, and this gave him some comfort.

After finishing his evening meal a few minutes later, he swatted his face in an attempt to kill the mosquito that had just taken a poke on his forehead. Unfortunately, as he moved his weapon, he nearly fell out of his hammock. He managed to grab and reposition it just in time. The next thing he did was find a comfortable position on his back after he closed his eyes and listened to the mysterious jungle noises while trying to figure out how far away they actually were from his camp. Eventually, he relaxed enough to fall asleep.

The next morning, just before breakfast, he did a radio check with the transmitter and receiver, which were stored in a waterproof container. He received word back from the submarine and then replied that he would check in again in forty-eight hours—after he had moved to the other side of the island.

Breakfast was another tin of meat, some nuts and raisins, and one of three apples he'd brought with him from the submarine's food supply. He also had two oranges, which he was looking forward to eating at some point, but as he ate the apple, he wondered if he could plant the seeds in some soil—if there was any soil. The island looked to be made entirely of sand so far, but there were many miles to explore. There had to be some soil somewhere. O'Brien figured that the birds would love an apple orchard. He took another bite and listened to the avian cacophony. How free those things sounded, singing and talking as the entire island woke up.

After thinking about the travel that he still had to do to reach his target on the other side of the island, Randy reached into his chest pocket and pulled out his map. Then, he got out of his hammock—cautiously—and walked over to his rucksack, where he unfastened an outside compartment and took out his compass. Once his map was opened up, O'Brien orientated his map to magnetic north. As he did so, a mosquito got him right on the neck, which caused him to stop what he was doing and smack it. "Bastard of a thing," he said, hoping that he'd killed the damn thing.

After tearing down his camp, the Australian moved out on his first bearing. He expecting things to be tough but it got much worse than he'd expected. There was saw grass that he had to go through—four meters high in some parts. When he was a quarter of the way through it, he stopped and took in some water from his canteen but some of the grass cut his exposed hands. Eventually, his canteen would need to be refilled with water that he could trust wouldn't make him sick. The water beneath the saw grass was several inches deep, which kept his feet wet. It wasn't clear and he wondered what kind of life lived in it. There was justifiable concern, given the water he had seen thus far.

By noon, O'Brien had meandered to the base of a hill but soon had to stop in his tracks. He'd spotted a viper resting on a thick vine that he was about to walk under. Carefully, he moved around the tree that the vines were dangling from. The leaf litter on the ground made him feel even more nervous as he made his way forwards. It was impossible to tell if there was anything hidden beneath it.

There were several inches of leaves on the ground, which were a great hiding spot for snakes, spiders, and other poisonous insects. He stopped after he had walked away from the trees where the snake was and took in the rest of the water that was in his canteen as the humidity did its best to ruin his day. It was slowing him down considerably, and he knew that he had to keep drinking down fluids or he'd become dehydrated in no time. Randy was lucky though because he still had another canteen, but besides his main objective, which was to reach one of the bays on the other side of the island, he also needed to find water before nightfall—and set up camp. There was no way he was going to make it all the way there in one night. He'd come to realize as much.

Another night in the middle of the island meant all sorts of discomforts, but that's what the commando had been expecting.

He put his pack up on a branch to keep it off the ground. It was already late in the afternoon, and he'd decided to stop for the night. He began to set up his hammock again, and after that was done, he took out a rag and soaked it with water from his canteen. The wet rag felt good as he rubbed his face clean with it.

When camp was set up, O'Brien decided to sit on his hammock and eat an orange. So far he hadn't seen any wild fruits that he could pick along the way, so he was pleased with his decision to have raided the galley on the submarine for as much fruit as he could carry. This had been a smart decision. Just before dark, the corporal took off his boots and put them on his hammock with him. Before he went to sleep, he wanted to clean between his toes and then clean his weapon to ensure that it would be in working order should he need to use it. As he worked away, washing the lint and grime from his feet, he came to the conclusion that the next day, he needed to find water and treat it so it would be usable.

At around two in the morning, though, he was awoken by something moving very slowly beneath him. It was scratching the dirt and seemed to be making some rather unusual noises—ones he'd never heard before. His reaction was swift as he sat upwards and put his flashlight beam of red light underneath where he was sleeping. There beneath him was the biggest crab he had ever seen in his life!

They were called coconut crabs, and they could climb trees. This one, with its legs fully stretched out, however, would reach almost four feet in diameter. It was a massive creature, and it would devour dead meat, but he wasn't dead and he still could move.

"Get! You scared the crap out of me, you bloody thing! Get out of here! Before I put you in a pot and eat you for dinner," the young commando said. That didn't do anything, so he took the bayonet that he had on his belt and poked at one of its pinchers, which were now sticking up in the air at him. When that didn't work, Randy took one of his boots and threw it at the thing, hoping it would force it to back away, which worked . . . partially. What O'Brien didn't expect was that the giant crustacean would grab onto one of his boots and drag it away into the jungle, never again to be retrieved.

O'Brien saw the mistake he'd just made and grabbed his other boot. He put it on the proper foot and then got out of his hammock and carefully hopped after the slow-moving crab, hoping to catch it before it disappeared into the dense bush. He only had one pair of boots, and if he lost one of them, life would become very bad for him.

When he saw the thing, he leaned forward as it backed up towards a tree. For a second or two, he had to play tug of war with the creature until it finally gave up and released his boot from its vice-like grip. When he got his boot back, he looked at the creature as it stared up at him in defiance. "Get away, you mongrel! Don't come back here or there'll be trouble."

The warning must have been understood because the large coconut crab moved away and slipped under some vegetation and was gone a few seconds later. Relieved to have recovered his stolen combat boot, O'Brien watched where he was walking and covered his exposed foot. Then, he walked back to his hammock and got back into it, hoping to doze off for a little longer.

Unfortunately for O'Brien, there were millions of mosquitos flying around him and he needed to get back under the bug net that he'd finally decided to use so he could get some protection. He looked at his pack with his flashlight. It was still there, and he was satisfied that he'd be okay where he was.

The birds woke him up at 5:30 in the morning. The entire island seemed to come alive at that time. Every creature in the jungle around him seemed to want to have a chat with something else that he couldn't see. It was like an alarm clock, and it was very reliable.

Giving up on sleep, he got out of his hammock and took it down. He put it in his pack and sorted out his gear. Then, he decided to boil some water, so he got out his metal canteen cup and used a fuel tablet to boil the water that he poured into it. While the water was on the boil, he looked at his map again under the light of his flashlight. O'Brien wasn't too far from the other side of the island, he soon discovered. If he hiked for the rest of the morning, he could make it over to the bay that he was supposed to observe and watch for enemy activity.

By 7 a.m., the commando had packed up his gear and was on the move again. He estimated that he'd be able to reach his objective in approximately five more hours. He wondered why it was still so dark when he took his first break several hours later. Then, he heard the sound of thunder and could almost smell the rain that was going to be unleashed on the island. The only good thing was that the winds were coming through the jungle since he was close to the other side of the island where the ocean was, and that was moving the hot humid air around him and making life a bit more tolerable as he put his canteen away. He hadn't come across any new sources of drinking water, and that meant that he only had a third of a canteen left before things went from bad to terrible. Hopefully, he'd find some more water as he got closer to the bay.

Luck was on his side, however, when he came across several jungle vines that were dangling from trees in front of him as he carefully traversed an abundance of leaf litter that covered the ground. He cut one of them and dangled one of the ends as he watched it drip out droplets of water. They weren't milky, which would have been a sign of poison. Instead, he saw clear fluid. He put some into the palm of his hand and tasted it. His tongue didn't go numb. This stuff was drinkable! He was elated and his morale shot through the roof.

It took him half an hour, but he managed to fill up both canteens, and with a smile on his face again, he wiped the sweat from his forehead and moved on as the rain started to penetrate the jungle canopy and fall to the ground, soaking every plant around him. Slowly, he moved through the green landscape. He was careful to avoid the vines, for fear of hidden vipers. They were so hard to see with their camouflage.

When the corporal finally made it to the other side of the island, his suspicions were proven correct. Coming through some thick foliage, he saw the bay out in front of him and was amazed by what it contained. There was a German U-boat unloading dozens of 55-gallon size oil drums! He was too far away to make out much else, though—especially with the rain coming down as it was.

Corporal O'Brien settled in to wait and to observe the area by covering himself with a poncho since the rain had not yet subsided. He looked around and saw a tree that he thought would work, so he took his time and climbed it, hoping he wouldn't slip and fall to the ground. When he reached the branch that gave him the best view, he stayed there for several hours as he watched what the Germans were doing.

Just as the sun was setting on the horizon though, O'Brien got a huge lesson about what other things lived in the trees. Suddenly, fire ants started biting his legs and ankles and they hurt tremendously! The pain was so intense that he chose to make a controlled fall using a vine that was close by. When he got to the ground, he immediately set to clean off his legs of ants and then gathered up his kit. He needed to find another place that was off the ground before he was caught in the pitch-black jungle. Randy didn't panic, though. Instead, he looked around to survey his options.

Suddenly, though he realized he had ants in his pants and they'd continued up to his crotch. The bites on his testicles and penis were more than he'd bargained for, and within seconds he'd undone his trousers and was killing every ant he could see until the biting finally stopped. After a minute of pure hell, Randy looked at his private parts to make sure he had suffered no permanent damage, and when satisfied that he'd be okay, he did up his pants. There were tears, though.

As the corporal looked off towards the bay he could see that he had perhaps another hour before the sun would disappear and he'd be encased in darkness. His decision was to move towards the bay for another fifteen minutes so that he was absolutely certain that there were no ant colonies near where he would set up his hammock for the night. He'd just learned a lesson that he never wanted to repeat.

The young Australian found a good place to set up about fifteen minutes later. As he looked around he saw that thorny bushes and bamboo now surrounded him, which hopefully would keep the pigs and coconut crabs away from him at night. Satisfied that this was a good place to set up camp, his next order of business was to make another shelter with his poncho so that the radio transmitter would be protected from the weather as he attempted to send a message out to the British submarine that he needed to check in with.

After setting up his poncho, he set to work assembling his radio transmitter set but was shocked to discover that the damn thing wasn't working. There was moisture all around it, which made him wonder if the rain had gotten inside and done some damage to it. "Shit," he said out loud as he looked at his fragile piece of equipment. O'Brien desperately wanted to send a message, and it had to be by Morse code. There was no other way to give an update to the British submarine that was supporting his mission.

While Randy tried to dry out his radio transmitter, he thought about his feet, which were blistered and causing him some discomfort. They'd been soaked for too long, and immersion foot was what he was now showing signs of having. The skin integrity was starting to be a problem for him, and soon it would show increasing signs of infection if he didn't get his boots and socks dry.

As he started to undo his boots to have a look at them, he thought about getting on with his mission but he couldn't see much at night anyway from where he was situated. Either the U-boat would still be there at first light or it wouldn't be. He had to take care of the radio set as well as his feet before he did anything else. Once he'd taken care of his feet, O'brien went to work setting up his hammock followed by the canvas rain cover that he'd made. It didn't take very long to have them both up, and soon he was protected from the elements. With those things taken care of, he could now think about eating something, but his menu selection wasn't great.

Later that night, while using his flashlight, the commando did his best to make notes of what he saw as he tried to make sketches of the events that he had seen thus far. He had some moonlight available, which allowed him to conserve his flashlight batteries. Some of the moonlight actually penetrated through the jungle canopy, giving it a very eerie, almost spiritual feeling. It also did something to the tides too because, for the past two full moons, fishermen had reported seeing navy vessels entering these waters and stopping by in the bays he'd been sent to observe.

By midnight, it started to rain some more, and Randy was thankful to have his canvas tarp protecting him from it all. The weather was relentless during the night and there weren't a lot of other noises from within the confines of the jungle. However, it was still quite dark when the corporal thought of a way to refill his water bottles by using the canvas rain cover to collect water for himself. Carefully, he slipped out of his hammock and reworked the angles of the canvas above his hammock. It only took an hour, and his canteens were both full, so now he didn't have to worry about finding water to drink the next day. The only other benefit from all that water coming down on him was that it also helped to lower the humidity a touch, which allowed him to sleep while under the protection of his canvas roof. When he finally settled back onto his hammock, the rain didn't touch him, and O'Brien managed to drift off to sleep.

The morning came early with the birds announcing their presence in the big trees. They had their priorities, and breakfast was on their minds. Randy had time for another apple, and then it was onto the day's festivities. He needed to test the radio set after he took down his hammock and rain cover and put everything in his rucksack.

First things first though, O'Brien checked his feet again before he tested his radio transmitter. The cracked skin between his toes was an open wound that would invite infection, but there were also some blisters that had broken on the bottom of his feet. This presented an opportunity to prove whether or not it was true that pissing on your blisters could take the pain away and heal them up quicker.

His sergeant had told him the trick in a hygiene class that he and several other commando course graduates were given before being sent out on missions around the pacific. There were no creepy-crawlies on the ground that he could see with the red light from his flashlight so he put his damp boots down onto the jungle floor. Then he got out of his hammock without falling out of it.

As he heard something in the jungle's canopy jumping from one branch to another, he put his feet into his boots and stood up straight. Then he took one foot out and put it on top of the empty boot and proceeded to piss all over it. It caused some stinging at first, and then the pain subsided a bit and he got on to other things like the radio set. He knew why he'd gotten the blisters. These boots hadn't been worn in enough before he'd taken them out on this mission. They were still pretty tight and hadn't completely moulded to his feet.

A short while later O'Brien was thrilled when his radio started working properly. "Holy Jesus, it works," said the corporal, who had a big smile on his face as he started to receive a message back in response to one he'd just sent out. He'd tried to send out three messages but no response had been received—until now. Focused as ever, the corporal went to work spilling out the details to whoever was working the radio room on the British sub.

After getting orders to continue observations, O'Brien needed to get on with his day. Help wasn't available for at least twenty-four to thirty-six hours, though. The skies were looking like they'd be clear, but with the winds he'd heard the previous night as he lay still in his hammock trying to sleep, anything could happen throughout the rest of the day.

As he looked at his radio set, he wondered if burying it was the right thing to do. The young corporal was going on patrol momentarily and so he had no other option available to him. How could he take a chance like that and leave his only means of communication out for somebody to find because it needed to dry out? He had his answer. Now he needed to find a good place to dig out so he would have the ultimate hiding spot for it.

By 6:30 in the morning, O'Brien had reached a good observation area of the Bay. The Nazi U-boat was still there, and there were people working on the beach, moving things that he couldn't yet identify. He wondered if they'd worked through the night. If so, they wouldn't want to be around for much longer, he figured as he took out his bino's to take a closer look. What he saw came as no surprise, though. The Germans were using slave labour to do the hard work for them.

He could see an enraged kraut yelling at their work party. He was screaming out orders and making wild gestures with his hands. Randy watched as a half dozen men took shovels and picks and then went off into the jungle. He needed to see what they were doing, so he moved off in a different direction because it was impossible to see what they were doing from where he was situated.

Instead of moving through the jungle, Randy did the sniper cat crawl on the beach just outside of where the jungle started to merge with the beach sand. He made great time and eventually found himself one hundred and fifty yards closer to his target. The U-boat was a new kind of German submarine that he'd not seen before in the many diagrams he had been shown by the people who had briefed him for the mission. This one seemed to have fuel pods welded onto the sides of it. Maybe that's what they were, he pondered, looking on curiously. He couldn't say for certain, but he drew a sketch of what he was looking at for future reference.

There was a shout in the distance, but Corporal O'Brien couldn't see anything. Then, the corporal saw that those same prisoners were now digging out a large pit, presumably to bury the drums. Never taking his eyes off the scene, he got into a better position from high up in a tree. Some of the men came back out onto the beach and put a barrel on a dolly. Then, two of them worked their way back to the jungle with it and they made their way back through the thick foliage just as several birds flew over them to find out what they were doing.

The young commando knew he needed to see where they were stashing their cargo. He had to get closer. As he looked around with his binoculars, another tree caught his attention. It had to be a thousand years old because its trunk was so enormous that it would be as wide as a middle-sized cow back at home. He slowly climbed down the tree that he was in, and when he reached the ground, he picked up his hidden pack and personal weapon before setting off in the tree's direction.

When Randy reached the other tree, he saw that the branches on it were big too. As he looked up and down the sides of it, he came to the conclusion that it could support his weight. Then he had a lightbulb moment and decided that it would also make an excellent observation post if he were to somehow get high enough.

After climbing the enormous tree, he soon saw what he'd suspected as he positioned himself into a prone position along a thick branch that was facing in the direction of the bay. As he looked through his bino's for a quick update on what was going on, he confirmed that he'd discovered a fuel dump. Observing these things on his very first mission made him feel pretty good inside.

By mid-afternoon, O'Brien needed to pinch himself to make sure this was all really happening. He suddenly felt rain hit one of his arms, and he looked up into the sky, only to see dark clouds moving towards the island. His thoughts were initially about his radio set. He wondered if it would remain dry, but he soon changed his focus to keep himself from getting soaked.

Randy carefully sat up and went back to the trunk of the tree. He was thirty feet off the ground, so he needed to be very careful. He reached up to his pack and opened it. He was careful not to put his hands inside it and waited for a few moments to pass. When nothing came out of it, he reached in and pulled out his poncho.

Off in the distance, there were sounds of thunder, and then he saw lightning. The wind started to pick up, and the leaves started to move against the wind as it hit the branches of the tree that he was on. As he observed the area in front of him, he could see many dark clouds that had appeared out of nowhere. The good thing about the rain as it came down hard was that it deterred the mosquitoes and lessened the humidity. For that saving grace, he was grateful as he sat still and observed the Germans until the sun began to set.

Eventually, he had to pee so he adjusted his body and went into a horizontal position. After relieving himself he looked over at his weapon, which was still hanging securely behind him on a different branch. Not falling out of the tree was quite the accomplishment, he thought.

For the remainder of the day, Corporal O'Brien stayed still and became a part of the landscape. When a small bird landed on the branch above to check him out, he felt like he was having a spiritual experience as he watched the bird looking at him closely. Eventually, it started chirping at him. It was nice to have a friend in such a lonely place. Fifteen minutes later, it flew away, satisfied that O'Brien meant him no harm.

With his poncho protecting him from the rain, Randy decided not to set up his hammock again as the night took over the island. Instead, he'd decided to just stay up in the tree as he watched the work party continue to move the barrels into the jungle. However, by 8 p.m., the Germans had finished their duties and boarded a skiff that took them back out to the U-boat. A short time later, he watched as the vessel headed out to sea under a high tide.

Corporal O'Brien knew that it was time to get closer because he needed to check out what they'd left behind. So, he made the decision to gather his kit and climb down the tree. He sat still at the base of it for a while and listened.

A short while later, Randy saw that the U-boat had successfully left the bay, and he started making his way along a game trail that he thought might get him to where they'd been burying their fuel. The raindrops were still falling from the leaves high in the canopy, and there wasn't a dry piece of clothing on his body as he moved along on his injured feet, trudging across the earth, which now was saturated and growing slick.

Unbeknownst to the Australian, the captain of the U-boat had ordered a message be sent to the Japanese submarine that was waiting to pick up what the Germans had just dropped off and hidden on that island. They were inbound, but he had no idea that this was happening. It wouldn't be long before somebody would be back for those barrels. He knew that much. Somebody needed them, but he had no idea when that might be, so he pressed on through the wet jungle landscape.

For now, though, the young Aussie was able to move forward through the darkness of the night to the buried German cache of fuel drums. The rainfall made it easier for him to prevent himself from being heard as he moved through the jungle as quietly as possible, ever on high alert for anything out of the ordinary. He used the W.O.W. technique that one of his instructors had taught him for observation in unfamiliar terrain.

His eyes were wide, tuned in to any potential movement—straight ahead and to both sides—as he slowly moved forward through thick vegetation. Peripheral vision was more important than his direct vision when traversing unfamiliar ground. That's what he'd been taught during his commando course, but under darkness, his eyes didn't really see anything. As a result, his heart rate increased because he wasn't sure what was off in the distance. He caught himself breathing rapidly as a result but managed to calm down. Randy went back to his combat breathing technique. He'd been trained to breathe in deeply for three seconds, to hold it for three seconds, and then to breathe it out for three seconds or longer. This would help him fill his brain and heart with oxygen so that he could make good decisions during periods of high stress when a person's thinking wasn't the best. The final thing he'd been taught was to keep walking, and those three things made up the W.O.W. fundamentals.

Suddenly, he saw a large spider moving through the debris on the ground in front of him. He had only seen it because he'd used the red light of his flashlight to look for a route forward. Ten feet ahead was a big green lizard attached to a tree trunk trying to be still so he wouldn't see it. Thankful that he hadn't walked right up to it in the pitch-black darkness Randy gave the large iguana a wide berth and let him continue on with his journey.

Eventually, Randy got to the well-camouflaged area that the prisoners had made, and soon he discovered the buried stash of drums by studying the ground with his flashlight as the rain continued to fall. It took him another ten minutes of looking around, but eventually, he stumbled across a pile of roots tossed behind a tree, and then he saw the flat earth covered over with leaves and other bits of debris to mask what was really there. He found where the Germans had buried the drums and started digging. Forty-five minutes later, O'Brien had dug up one of the containers and was ready to take a look at what was inside it.

"Strange. Not aluminium. Not tin, neither," he muttered to himself as he moved more dirt from around the container. Whatever metal they were made from was heavy, though, he thought. The commando grabbed his pliers from his pant pocket and used them to pry away at the lid. It didn't want to budge.

He put more effort into it, and suddenly it popped open. The lid came up with a wet suction sound. Liquid mercury splashed up over the lips of the barrel, spilling onto the ground and all over one of his arms and onto his pants.

"Shit," he said. The commando scrambled to keep the barrel from falling over on its side with great difficulty, but he just managed to keep it upright. Randy saw that the liquid that was moving around was quite slow and sloppy. Then, he realized what he was looking at. "Mercury? Bloody Hell! Wasn't expecting *that* to be here," he said.

A few minutes later, he made short work of sealing the container up again and worked to put it back into the ground. He took his time covering the area back up and putting things back as he had found them. When he left the area, you couldn't tell anyone had been there.

Concerned that he was covered with something quite sinister, Corporal O'Brien walked back out onto the beach and then went into the ocean to wash himself off. This was the best he could do to decontaminate his body for the moment. He hoped he wouldn't be seen and did his best to maintain a low profile as he crawled out onto the sand and hid behind a log, staring out at the breakers of a reef that wasn't too far away. That U-boat had to have been careful coming in and possibly couldn't do it at any other time other than on a full moon when the king tides came to the island. That would allow the ship to come in over the reef safely, he thought as he noticed a rip in his pants just below the knee on his left leg. He needed to get that stitched up when he could.

The rain had almost stopped completely by now, thankfully, but the humidity was still present. When Randy was satisfied that he'd washed off the mercury from his skin, he walked back to get under the cover of the trees so as to prevent himself from being seen from the air or another boat. When he managed to find his way back to where he'd hidden his radio, he suddenly heard the sounds of pigs and nearly tripped over some roots. At some stage, these pigs had been introduced to this rather large island in the middle of nowhere. There were animal tracks as well as holes dug into the ground as he looked around. It was all a good indication that pigs were in the area.

O'Brien observed the ground and determined that multiple animals on the island had worn the earth into a hard rut. His red filtered light illuminated the way as he walked underneath the jungle canopy. The corporal wondered if there would be any future health problems because of being splashed with the mercury. He didn't know a great deal about the stuff, but he did know that human skin absorbed it quite easily and that it stayed in the body forever. Was it a heavy metal? He wasn't sure. That thought worried him as he stopped to listen to the animals snorting off in the distance as the stars started illuminating the sky above him and the cloud cover started to dissipate above the jungle.

By a stroke of luck, there were no other surprises on the way back to his hideaway. A quick check of the area revealed that no one had been rooting through the debris on the ground, which covered the stash spot for the radio set. O'Brien pulled out his entrenching tool and began digging up his buried radio, which was protected by a sheet of canvas and a top cover of bamboo. When he finally got it out from the hole he'd dug, he set it up on a rock, using his flashlight to guide him to it safely.

After he was sure it was safe there, he then took a water break and listened attentively for anything out of the ordinary. His water bottle was soon empty, but in the morning, he would go to the stream he had discovered along the way back and refill both of the bottles that he had brought with him.

Worrying that it might start to rain later during the night once more, Randy went to work setting up his poncho over the radio again. There was no question that he was tired, but he forced himself to push on so he could send out another message because this one communication was possibly the biggest thing he'd ever contribute to the war effort.

Unfortunately, he quickly learned that the damn thing wasn't about to cooperate for him. Some moisture may have gotten into it again, even though it had been in a waterproof container. He'd have to give it another thorough cleaning, he thought as he contemplated which parts he should inspect first. Slowly and methodically, he checked over every inch of the radio just to make sure.

The commando was pretty confident that nobody was there on the island but him. Could he chance having a fire? No, absolutely not. Instead, he set to work rubbing it down with a clean cloth. When he was finished cleaning it, he tried it again, and this time, it seemed to work. He attempted to send out a message but it wasn't at the scheduled check-in time so he didn't receive a response. He waited for a short time and then finally concluded that nobody was within range, so he reluctantly decided to call it a night and go and get some well-earned shuteye.

Before he set up his hammock, though, he decided to look in the bushes around where he was going to sleep. Randy wondered if that giant coconut crab would show up and try and take his stuff. When he didn't see any signs of it, he made sure his pack was hanging securely on a branch and that his weapon was close by should it be needed.

O'Brien then checked to make sure that his canvas tarp that was above his hammock was secure from all angles, and when he was sure that it was, he placed his backside upon the hammock and undid his boots. His feet ached, which required a look-see before he crashed for the night. The skin was white on their undersides and looked to be healing, but he gave them a quick cleaning anyway and got the junk out from between the toes. Finally, he dried off each foot with the triangular bandage that he had wrapped around his neck.

When he was satisfied that he'd done enough for them, he put on the fresh pair of clean socks that he'd pulled out from his pack and put them on his feet. Then, he laid down and brought his boots up with him so that no creepy crawlies would get into them while he slept. He didn't want to eat the tinned meat, but he was hungry, so he took the last orange and started removing the peel. When he tasted the first piece of the fruit, he found it to be delicious.

It wasn't easy getting to sleep for him. For quite some time, he just listened to the many noises that were being made in the surrounding darkness. Several small animals ran through the undergrowth not far away from camp, and that really spooked him because he couldn't see anything due to it being so dark. Eventually, however, he did manage to close his eyes and drift off. For several hours he slept soundly.

However, a pig squealing and running off in the nearby jungle woke him up at four in the morning. He sat up on high alert and fell out of his hammock. The first thing he did was search for his flashlight so he could see if there were any snakes or scorpions near him on the ground. After he found it, he went to work recovering his Thompson and then his boots.

When he was sure that it wasn't a Japanese patrol, he settled back into his hammock. His feet hadn't bothered him at all through the night so it appeared that peeing on your blisters actually had some merit to it. The last pair of dry socks felt so great on his feet, and in a couple of hours, he'd put his feet back in those boots and get back to the mission. As he tried to relax one more time, he heard droplets of rain starting to hit the leaves in the trees and bushes that were around his hammock. Sleep came, though, and soon he was dreaming again.

The birds were on time with their wake up call at 5:30 a.m. The shrieks that he heard got him up, and he began his morning by removing his clean socks and pissing on his feet one last time before he did his boots up. Then came drying them off, which was followed by a radio check. He hoped that the poncho had done its job and that the radio set would work. He'd find out soon enough, but for the moment, he needed to tear down camp.

After packing up his hammock and taking down the canvas tarp that was hanging over it, he went over to the radio set and started sending out another message. It was frustrating. He was sending out Morse code, but nobody seemed to be replying to him. He kept trying, though, hoping somebody might be listening.

And then, to his amazement, he got a reply from the British submarine. He was elated! It came as no great surprise that the British sub wanted him to set up some kind of an observation post so that, come the next full moon, they'd be ready to attack the next U-boat that came into the bay. Those were his new orders.

With the radio check-in complete, Corporal O'Brien decided it was time to eat something else. He opened up a can of bully beef and mixed it with some curry powder that he'd brought along with his personal stuff. It didn't taste half bad when you put heat into it, he thought, as he took his first bite. Randy took his time eating it up with the help of some biscuits, but for dessert he ate an apple, and it tasted fantastic. He was happy to have loaded himself up with so much fruit prior to disembarking from the submarine.

After his morning meal, the Australian felt the call of nature, so he looked for a spot where he could dig a hole and take a dump, which he had to do carefully so as not to step on any poisonous insects. He knew the British Sub was on other missions to resupply the Coastwatchers on the other islands nearby, but with some luck, they'd be able to destroy whatever submarine or boat came to pick up the mercury. It was a welcome relief to know that he had people out there who would come to his aid if he needed assistance.

Once again, he focused on the task of hiding his radio. This time, he was more careful and placed pieces of split bamboo beneath the radio and along the sides of the hole, and more on top of it. Then, he covered that with a spare piece of canvas that he'd cut up for further protection and began putting dirt on top of it until the hole was filled back in completely. After he had sprinkled debris all over the area, he decided to venture out to the beach to take a look around. He did his boots up and then grabbed his rucksack. When the Aussie had it on firmly, he picked up his weapon and headed out of the jungle, returning to the bay where the Nazi sub had been the day before.

As O'Brien moved through the jungle, he was distracted by the sounds of the crashing waves off in the distance, which caught his attention, but they were still quite far away from where he was. One of his priorities was the refilling of his water bottles, so Randy headed to the stream that he'd discovered the previous day. When he got to it, he found that the water was flowing, so the water wasn't stagnant. Even so, he knew that he had to put water tablets into the bottles to kill all the microscopic parasites that might do him harm.

While the tablets worked their magic, the corporal sat on a rock at the stream and became a part of the natural surroundings, watching the birds fly around the trees above him. It was an awesome place to relax, and he felt good just sitting there as he watched the wind move the leaves of the elephant ear plants that were all over the place just above the ground. Then, Randy remembered that he'd also brought his two pairs of socks and a shirt to wash and get clean, so he set to work and started washing his clothes. When they were done he carefully laid them out onto a rock so the sun could dry them out.

A short time later, he continued forward as he searched for a better place to observe the bay from. When he thought he'd reached such a place, he sat near several trees and observed the ocean for any signs of German or Japanese activity. For many hours, he stayed motionless and watched the area for signs of enemy movement, but nothing disturbed his view.

When the sun began to set, Corporal O'Brien went back to his hidden camp and made himself an evening meal of tinned beef and biscuits. He cleaned his Thompson and made sure that it was functional. When he was satisfied that it was, O'Brien took care of some personal hygiene with water that he'd brought back with him from the stream.

Then came a night full of noises, but he managed to sleep until around three in the morning, when that same wild pig woke him up, deciding to test him by running by his camp again. It startled the corporal, but he knew it was an animal and not a person, so with his heart still racing, he settled back down into the hammock and smacked a mosquito off of his forehead as he waited for sleep to overcome him once again.

Come dawn, the forest was an entirely different place. Birds could be heard calling out to the world. Soft, loamy blanketed the plants around his camp. It looked like it was an entirely different place from the one where the Australian had fallen asleep. Randy got up and looked down at the ground. He didn't see any critters, so he put his boots down beneath him and then got out of his hammock.

It didn't take long for the commando to tear down and pack up. O'Brien's new plan was to move camp a bit closer to the bay area, and the first course of action was to move some of his kit over to the spot that he wanted to try out.

As he did his best to navigate through the tropical jungle that surrounded him, he kept a close eye on his compass to ensure that he was heading in the right direction. Sometimes the vegetation was so thick where he was that he was unsure if he was heading in the right direction. With the advancing light, he looked for landmarks that he knew were out there—such as a giant stone that wasn't far away from the stream where he had refilled his water bottles the previous day. There were several big tall dead trees that had fallen over as well, and when he came across one of them, he was pretty sure he knew that he was headed in the right direction.

As Randy walked through the jungle slowly, he noticed several birds situated up in the trees ahead of him fly off into the sky but made nothing of it. Then, his peripheral vision picked something up to his left. He saw movement. Quickly, he got down onto one knee and hid behind a bush. He couldn't see what it was, but he was now well hidden. Carefully, he took his pack off and held his weapon at the ready with the safety catch now off.

For several long minutes, he stayed still and just listened to his surroundings. His instructor at the commando school had taught him that Special Forces required eyes like an owl, ears like a deer, and the nose of a wolf. Right now, he was using all of his senses to try to figure out what was up ahead of him. The humidity of the morning was stifling, but he decided to move forwards. He could still hear whatever it was, but it didn't seem like it was behaving as a human would be. His curiosity was getting the better of him and he knew it. After putting his safety catch back onto safe mode, O'Brien slowly crept closer through the several yards of saw grass until he stopped and watched what was moving up ahead. For twenty minutes, he didn't move a muscle, and then, finally, he saw that it was the wild pig that had been harassing his campsite. It was looking for food again.

He relaxed his arms and let his SMG point to the ground. "I wouldn't mind some bacon Mr Piggy but not today. We're too close to the target and we don't want to make any noise," he said, almost laughing.

With his guard down, Randy turned around and started walking back to where he'd left his pack. As he went back through the saw grass, he looked up at the clear blue skies and wondered how long the clear weather would last. Eventually, he got back to his rucksack and put it on. Then, he took out his canteen and had a big drink before pushing off again.

The Australian continued forwards through the jungle landscape, moving on the bearing that he knew would get him to the right place. When he reached the second fallen tree an hour later, he looked around at the surrounding bush with his peripheral vision like he'd been taught, and nothing was detected, so he took off his rucksack and rested. As he sat on the fallen tree, he didn't notice two areas of grass suddenly move behind where he was sitting.

A moment later, it was too late for him. The two Japanese soldiers charged at him with their rifles and bayonets pointed in his direction. They quickly overpowered the corporal and put him face-down on the ground while a third Japanese soldier climbed down from another nearby tree. Randy was caught off guard and didn't stand a chance.

O'Brien had been caught with his dick in the wind, and now he would pay a severe price for not seeing his enemy hiding in wait for him. Soon, several more Japanese soldiers came out from the jungle and surrounded the nearby area, hoping to capture or kill more Australian soldiers, and while they waited to ambush, one of them put a gunnysack over Randy's head so he couldn't see anything else.

The Japanese soldiers then bound his wrists with thick, coarse rope as a gun barrel pressed between his shoulders. They stood him up and then marched the Australian through the jungle, down a section of trail that he hadn't yet ventured into. As they walked along the unfamiliar terrain, Corporal O'Brien tripped several times and fell to the ground. The Japanese soldier that was in front of him, who was also holding the end of the rope that connected to Randy's neck, only yanked him along faster while the soldiers behind him poked him in his ass with their bayonets, which stung each time they jabbed him.

The Japanese spoke loudly to each other, but the young commando wasn't able to pick out anything that they were saying. O'Brien knew that he was in deep trouble, and his mind was trying to figure a way out of this mess when he was hit in his lower back by a rifle butt, giving him a message to hurry up.

For some time, they travelled through the jungle until they could all hear the crashing ocean waves that were hitting the coral reefs just off of the island. In another circumstance, the beach might have been idyllic. Seeing those waves crash against the shoreline could help a person think through their problems. The sun was pleasant when they weren't going through the jungle, and if Randy had a girl with him, this would be one hell of a place to fool around as the sun was sinking.

Unsure what his fate would be, the Australian had no option but to go along with his captor's whims. The rope was passed off to another soldier. They led him along the beach, up to the bay where a rowboat was visible. Off in the distance outside of the bay was a Japanese submarine. Since the tide was still too low for the sub to come into the bay, they had sent a shore party to determine if anyone else was hiding out on the island.

One of the guards removed the gunnysack from his head, and O'Brien could breathe much easier. He was shocked to see the Japanese submarine and wished he had been able to report its discovery. The corporal hoped that the British sub would come to his rescue and blow the shit out of that Japanese vessel, but he was quickly distracted from his thoughts when he was poked in the thigh with another bayonet strike and ordered to go off into the jungle again, this time heading towards the buried fuel drums.

When he got to the area where they had been buried, he saw two other allied prisoners of war who were already well on their way to digging up the cache of fuel drums. A screaming Japanese soldier then pointed, and Randy got the message that he was to assist them and quickly got to work. While he started moving dirt, he wondered when and how the others had been captured. He locked eyes with both of the other prisoners, and on several occasions, they acknowledged each other but said nothing out loud. No doubt, they had been picked up on some other island in the Pacific, O'Brien thought.

Their guards kept up a constant string of dialogue between each other and made many jokes about having stuck O'Brien in the ass with their bayonets. They didn't seem to be worried about his health, and as he looked down his legs, he could see many streams of dry blood caked around his ankles. He noticed that his boots felt soggy, and that must have meant they were waterlogged from all of the blood that was coming out of his stab wounds, which he guessed must have been at least nine different injury sites on his ass cheeks and from his legs.

It took until late afternoon for the barrels to all be pulled up out of the holes. Shortly thereafter, the prisoners were lined up in a straight line as a senior Japanese soldier walked behind them muttering insults. They all knew that hell was about to be unleashed upon them in some tragic way, but they couldn't do anything about it. Soon, a Japanese naval officer came out of the jungle and approached them. He had come up from the beach and had presumably just arrived from the Japanese sub. Randy noticed that attached to his side was a katana, which the officer held firmly with one hand so that it was easier for him to move around.

The Japanese officer was younger than O'Brien. He walked up to him and said, "Who are you? What is your mission? You tell me now or you die!"

The commando stayed quiet for a few seconds. Then he said his name, his rank, and his serial number, which enraged the young lieutenant.

"What country are you from?" The officer continued.

"Australia, mate. We're prisoners of war. Geneva convention. We have rights."

The Japanese officer laughed. "Japanese no sign the Geneva convention, idiot!" Then, he looked at all three prisoners as he unsheathed his katana from its scabbard. He threatened all three of them with it and then shouted an order to two Japanese guards who stood behind the prisoners. They immediately walked over to O'Brien and hit him with rifle butts below the knees causing him to fall to the ground. They then grabbed both of Randy's arms and made him bow his head. "You bastard!" The Aussie said defiantly. "This isn't right, mate. You're a piece of shit, you fucking mongrel!"

The officer stood over him and screamed, "I am no mongrel. You are a spy! We kill spies. You talk or you die. Talk!" He ordered one last time.

When Corporal O'Brien stared out at the Japanese Submarine in defiance, it infuriated the Japanese Lieutenant, who said another command to the two guards. They quickly grabbed his arms and tied them behind his back. When that was done, the Japanese officer walked over to O'Brien's side, raised his sword, and came down with a lightening fast blow, which severed Randy's head from his shoulders.

His lifeless body started spurting blood in every direction, and the two other prisoners were filled with indescribable anger. Also scared beyond description, they were then forced to go back to work moving the barrels of mercury toward the waterline. The young commando's lifeless body lay motionless under the hot tropical sun.

Chapter 1

After months of training in Northern Scotland, Cpl. Babcock was being tested again for his ability to think and perform while working alone in severe weather conditions. The wind was brutally bad out on the open ice in the mountain range that Carl was traversing, but he was totally focused, fearful that he might fall through a snowy ice covering that prevented him from seeing a crevice. In the back of his mind, he was using another important lesson that had been taught to him while on the selection course—the acronym S.T.O.P.A., which he was supposed to think about whenever he was in dire circumstances. It stood for 'Stop, Think, Observe, Plan, and Action.' As he looked around the area in front of him, he was doing just that as he tried to select a safer route. The cold weather was making it harder for Carl to think things through properly, but luckily he recognized this fact and was trying to do a better job at problem-solving.

With the mountain peaks above him, Babcock knew he was in some kind of a naturally made air funnel, as the wind blew ferociously around him, spraying a fine mist of ice crystals into his face and dropping the outside temperature even further. He didn't trust the route that he had chosen any longer, which is why he was poking holes into the ice as he climbed upwards. The corporal needed to get up and over the ridge but his initial idea of getting there seemed more dangerous now. Carl wanted to find a better way to reach his next objective, which he had to reach on his own merits. With less than nine hours to go, he had to make up for lost time after choosing a bad route the previous day as well.

Thirty yards later, Babcock discovered what he had been dreading. There was a buried crevice hiding just in front of him, and if he hadn't kept doing the prodding with his stick that he carried along with him, Carl would now be down a blue icy hole that he'd never be able to climb out of. He unleashed a string of profanities and used the combat breathing method he'd been taught to slow his heart rate down and give his brain the oxygen it needed in order to make better decisions as he looked around. A few minutes later when things seemed a bit clearer for him, the corporal's decision was to walk backwards, seeking his own tracks to step back into.

Stiff and sore, Corporal Babcock continued to look at the ice and snow around his feet as he visually searched every inch of the ground before moving back a step. Slowly and methodically, he moved away from the area as the weather did everything it could to slow him down.

Two hours later, Carl had finally made it up to the top of the ridge and looked out over it. He was in darkness, but there was still so much he could still see thanks to the moonlight that reflected up from the snow. He took the time to figure out the direction of travel that he needed to take as he looked down into the valley below him. The wind hit his face and made it numb but the SAS candidate had to find a route down to the bottom of the other side of the mountain. Yet, everywhere he looked, it all seemed so desolate and foreboding. How could people have lived up in Northern Scotland? The weather up there was brutal! He put his compass and map back into his midcoat pocket and started thinking that he might be looking at the first leg of the descent that might actually work out for him. Meanwhile, he remained aware of the stressful situation that he was facing with so many elements working against him at that particular moment.

As Babcock walked up the hard crusty snow on the ridge, he started to lose his footing to the slippery ice that had formed underneath it. His mind was full of lessons, and he decided to try one of the tips the instructors had given to the candidates before they'd been sent off on their own. The suggestion Sergeant Mitchell had given them was to put socks over one's footwear if you had nothing else to help you get a better grip on the ice. So, Carl took off his pack and then removed one of his gloves. He opened up one of the side pockets and took out a pair of socks.

After putting them over the tips of his boots he then put on his glove and did the side pocket back up. Carl then opened up the main compartment, pulled out a rope for his descent, and then did it back up again. With the pack back on, he started out afresh, and this time, he made progress thanks to the socks binding on the snow and the ice as he walked over to the side of the mountain that he needed to go down. Mitchell had been right, which amused Babcock to no end! It was another affirmation about how many things you could actually do with a pair of socks! *What an amazing trick*, he thought as he forged on, trying to make up lost time.

Before starting down the other side of the mountain, Babcock checked his compass once again and took a bearing on a river that was frozen over down in the valley where he needed to go. Careful not to slip, he took his time under the moonlight and used the hundred-foot rope to help him descend fifty feet at a time. The snow anchor was tricky to do because it involved packing a lot of snow down hard and then weaving the rope around it so that two ends both dangled over the side of the mountain. Then, when he had gone the first fifty feet, he could pull the entire rope down and start again with another snow anchor.

Babcock slipped several times along the way, which made him think about his perception of fear. He could easily fall and die on this descent, but each time he lost his confidence, he regained it again. To do so, he would remind himself that the mistakes he had made hadn't killed him and that he needed to recover from each one, remember to do his combat breathing, and make good decisions on his next move. Each time he repeated that process, it helped him regain his confidence and belief that he could get down that mountain on his own merits.

It took him several hours to complete the full descent, but he got down the mountain in one piece. His last close call had been the scariest, when he'd lost his footing and several rocks had come loose, almost causing him to fall. Luckily, the snow anchor had done its job and he'd been okay.

After reaching the bottom of the mountain, it was still dark and the wind wasn't relenting one bit. He took his gloves off one by one and inspected his hands closely because he had little feeling in them. They were numb but functional. Though he had many layers on his torso, he felt unable to get warm and immediately thought of the idea to start doing some burpees to get the blood moving to his extremities. The exercise made you warm up fast, and after a minute of doing those, he was good to go. After readjusting his rucksack and checking his bearing again with his compass, he continued onwards through the valley that he was now situated in.

It took Carl another forty-five minutes to reach the frozen river. As he studied the landscape, he wondered if it would hold his weight if he attempted to cross the ice. He wasn't prepared for the potential repercussions, so he looked for exposed water that he could assess the depth of so he could possibly cross that and get over to the other side. Time was ticking, and he needed to do something quick.

After hiking 300 yards upriver, which was away from the mountain he'd just come down, he saw broken ice, wet saturated snow, and some exposed water that hadn't refrozen overnight. That told Carl that it wasn't as cold down where he was as it had been way up on the mountains that he had just come over. Putting his walking stick into the river, he learned that the depth of water was anywhere from two to four feet.

He couldn't be sure exactly how deep it was in the middle, so he decided to take off his clothes and put them into his bag. This was the ancient method of crossing rivers in the winter under arctic conditions. The next thing he would need would be a fire on the other side, but he would be so cold from the freezing water that he might not be able to start one if he was shivering uncontrollably, which was why he had already made a fire bundle and had kept it in one of his side pouches of his Bergen. He removed the bundle from his pack and placed it on a large piece of bark. It was freezing-cold being naked, so he quickly started the fire and rejoiced at the heat he was already feeling. Then, he put his clothes and boots in his pack. Putting it on his shoulders, he then took his weapon and his walking stick and started moving into the flowing water.

His body didn't like the feeling of the freezing water, but he went in up to his knees. Lucky for him, the water where he was only went up to mid-thigh, but it was deep enough to carry him away under the ice that was further along down the river. If that happened, his body wouldn't be seen again.

As Carl dismissed the thought, he reached back to shore and yanked at the piece of bark, which he had tied to a piece of string and fastened to his belt so he could pull it along six feet behind him. Then, making a triangle formation with his legs and the walking stick, Babcock faced upstream and shuffled one foot at a time over to the other side. First, he planted the stick at the river bottom firmly. Then, he moved a foot closer to the other side. It was just a matter of repeating the process.

Carefully, the corporal looked back and saw that his fire was smoking wonderfully. He looked forward to using that fire to reheat his body when he got to the other side safely. Suddenly, the freezing water hit his testicles, though, and that distracted his attention immediately. "Jesus Christ," he said in utter shock as the river water soaked his midsection. Then, he remembered to focus on his breathing instead and to reaffirm his goal, which was to cross the river and get to the other side. Two minutes later, he managed to do it.

After leaving the river, Babcock climbed up through the snow until he was on solid ground. Then, he took off his pack and put down his walking stick and his rifle on top of it. Next, he turned around and retrieved the piece of bark that had his fire on it. It was smoking wonderfully, and there were some small flames showing.

The corporal took the fire up over the side of the river and put it down on a flat area after kicking the snow away from it. Carl then saw a tree nearby and ran over to the area underneath it that had no snow. As his eyes scanned the ground, he saw what he was looking for. There was dry bark and a broken branch at the base of the tree that had broken away. He retrieved those items and took them back to the fire. While shivering, the SAS candidate broke it all up and put it over the fire, then left it to burn while he went back to the side of the river to retrieve his stuff.

The weather must have been many degrees below zero, he thought as he started pumping off pushups to warm up his body to be nimble enough to get all of his clothes back on. As he opened his Bergen, the corporal saw that his clothing had remained dry. He quickly took out his boots and stepped into them so his feet were out of the snow, and then he pulled out his shirt and sweater, which went on right away. Next came his long underwear and then his pants. It felt good to get his clothes back on his body as he heard the crackle of a burning fire off in the distance behind him.

It didn't take long for him to finish putting on his socks and doing his boots up. The last thing he put on was his toque, but he was still shivering uncontrollably, which meant that he was experiencing a mild form of hypothermia. Babcock's solution was to pull out his canteen cup and fill it with the water from the river. Then he walked over to the fire and as he did so, he saw several more sticks that he thought he could burn, so he picked them up too and took them back with him to the fire. A few moments later, he was seated before the flames, which lifted his mood considerably as he placed his canteen cup down. When that was taken care of, Carl broke up the sticks that he'd collected and put those on the burning wood, which was emitting some welcome heat in his direction. For a moment, he enjoyed the feeling of warmth on his hands as he held them close to the flames.

While the corporal got his body temperature back up, off in the distance, a lone man surveyed Carl through a pair of binoculars. The smoke from his fire had been spotted. It was Sergeant Mitchell and he was making a mental note of what he was looking at. He could see the smoke from the fire and the man stoking the flames. Mitchell wondered if the candidate would make it to the rendezvous point in time because Babcock still had ten miles of snow to navigate through before he reached the next checkpoint that he was supposed to get to.

As he looked on, Sergeant Mitchell thought about Babcock crossing the freezing river naked and started laughing. He knew that wouldn't have been very pleasant.

When Corporal Babcock finally did get to his next objective, the sun was starting to set, which made it harder to find the exact spot where the support staff was situated. It had started snowing, and Carl didn't see Sergeant Mitchell until Corporal Babcock was almost walking over his shelter. When he did see the person that was waiting for him, he stood there for a moment and wondered if he was really seeing someone sitting on a piece of log underneath a tarp. Before he could say anything, though, Sergeant Mitchell spoke out in French and said, "What's your number?" Babcock was confused. Then, he told him that he was number thirty-three. Sergeant Mitchell looked up at the corporal from inside his shelter and looked him over. He could sense that Babcock was confused because of the freezing weather, and he wanted to observe what the corporal would do under stress.

He reached over to his Bergen and pulled out his weapon so Carl could see it. It was a gleaming machine gun. "You were on the range with it last week, and you passed with a decent score. I want you to go over there and strip down this weapon. Any questions?"

Babcock knew the weapon well, but his mind wasn't thinking properly. "No questions, staff," he replied in French as he took the weapon from the Special Forces instructor and walked over to a place in the snow a few feet from where Mitchell could watch him strip his weapons. But he figured that he would have to assemble the weapon as well. To do so required taking off his gloves. It was really cold, and Carl wondered how long it would be before his fingers failed him. He tried not to think about it too much, though, and put his pack down on the ground. Then, he knelt beside it and used the pack as a makeshift table so he wouldn't lose any parts from the weapon in the snow.

It took him three minutes to do it. When Sergeant Mitchell was satisfied that he'd done the job properly, he asked him what the effective range of a nine-millimetre round was. It took Babcock a second or two to remember the answer, but he provided the right one. Sergeant Mitchell nodded and then told him to put his weapon back together, which Babcock did.

Mitchell was poker-faced as he took the SMG back from the corporal. Carl had a moment, so he began putting his gloves back on while he watched the NCO put the weapon inside his shelter and made sure it was protected from the elements outside of his shelter. Babcock was still outside and was being exposed to stormy weather while the SAS selection NCO reached into his coat and pulled out his notebook. He opened it up to a page that had several grid references on it.

The sergeant looked up at the SAS candidate, who by then was shivering. "I want you to take out your map and show me what's located at grid reference 639123."

Babcock had just started warming up his hands again but quickly shut out the pain of his entire body as he took off one glove and opened up the jacket pocket where he kept his map. He took it out and looked at it. Then, he realized he'd already forgotten the grid reference. "Can you say it one more time for me, please, staff?"

Sergeant Mitchell looked at Corporal Babcock and repeated himself as he watched the candidate pull out a pencil so he could write it down. "The grid reference is 639123," he replied as the corporal nodded and quickly scribbled it out in the notebook he'd just pulled out from his chest pocket. He took off his jacket and put it over his head so he could have some protection from the wind. He took out his flashlight and shined it on his map. His fingers found the grid square on the map, and then he saw the lake on the map. He took his jacket off of his head and looked back at the senior NCO. "I believe it's a lake, Sergeant," Babcock replied.

Mitchell looked Babcock over and then nodded. He reached into his pack. Carl thought the sergeant was going to offer him something to eat or drink or perhaps give him another grid reference to head off towards, but instead, he pulled out a nine-millimetre pistol, cocked it, and then pointed it right in his face. "How the hell do I know you're number thirty-three? You didn't ask me for the bloody password. What's the password you were told to say when you saw me?" Corporal Babcock knew that he'd just stuffed up, and for all he knew, he'd just failed the course. Several months' worth of hard training had come down to this moment and he'd just made a serious mistake.

Mitchell got up and stepped out from his shelter while still pointing the pistol towards the corporal. "Put your hands up, you idiot. You've just finished this phase of the course. Do you understand? How do I know who you are without the right password? Never forget that if you're out in the field and you're all alone—say you need to meet up for resupply—you need a password, idiot! Now turn around. Do you understand that this phase of the course is over?" Babcock nodded as he knelt on the ground. The sergeant then put a sandbag over his head and tied the back of his hands with cordage.

"You're now a prisoner of war. Don't you fucking move," he screamed at Babcock. He then took out a whistle and blew it loudly. Soon, Carl could hear several men approaching, and then he was suddenly lifted up by both arms and escorted for several hundred yards to a parked truck. The only good thing was that he was out of the snow, but it was still quite cold inside the back of the vehicle.

There were several minutes of silence before several other men climbed into the back of the truck. Carl made the mistake of talking, and as a consequence received a rifle butt from a Lee Enfield Mk 4 into the middle of his left thigh, which hurt like hell. The Charlie horse it gave him caused him a lot of pain, but he said nothing. While he was trying to recover from the injury, someone got into the front of the vehicle and it soon roared to life. The next phase of selection was going to be the interrogation phase. As the truck moved slowly through the snow, Carl tried to prepare himself for whatever was to come.

Three hours later inside the building that he'd been put into, Carl was wondering what was going on. The staff on the 5th S.A.S. selection course were out to cause as much pain and discomfort as was possible. He still had the sandbag over his head, which was hard to breathe through. Babcock needed to adjust his body periodically because there was no heat in the room that he was in, making movement necessary to stay warm. And yet each time he tried to move his body out of the stress position that they told him to stay in, somebody would come from behind him and put him into a different position. So even though there was silence, it was obvious that somebody was constantly watching his every move.

There were moments when he could hear the course staff members berating other people for moving around in other rooms as he remained blindfolded in the stress position that he had been put into with his hands up against the wall and his legs three feet away from it. That was the first sign for him that he wasn't alone in the building. It now seemed as though there were other candidates that had also made it to this last phase of the course. He had heard through the grapevine—before he even started—that most people quit during the interrogation phase of selection, but he had resolved himself not to be one of those people, no matter what was thrown his way.

That being said, by midnight Babcock was almost ready to concede. Nothing he'd been through had prepared him for this level of intensity. He chased the idea out of his mind, though, when two soldiers came into his room. They untied the cordage that still held his hands behind his back and picked him up off the ground by both arms. The relief was incredible as the blood ran back into his hands and fingers. Carl found it difficult to walk, though, so the staff members had to drag him into another room.

Carl still had the blindfold on and then one of the selection staff placed a sandbag over his head, making it difficult to breathe. He was put onto a chair, and he heard people walking around him. Somebody kicked his feet. Another hit him in the back of the head. "What's your name, rank, and serial number, soldier?" one of the men asked, but he remained silent and kept his head facing down.

Somebody pushed his chair backwards causing him to fall. Staying on the ground, he mentally prepared himself for the beating he expected to come at any moment.

"What's your name, rank, and serial number, you bloody idiot?" another man shouted as he bashed a wooden handle of some kind against the wall. Carl was getting scared. "You're a spy. You know what we do with spies? There are no rules. Now tell us what unit you're with? What country do you originate from?"

The corporal said nothing, and after hearing several more sounds of the wooden handle hitting the cement floor beside his ear and feeling it poke his shoulders, he was suddenly shocked by cold water being poured over his face, which was covered by the sandbag. At first, he sputtered and tried to remove the sandbag but then somebody picked him up and put him back into the chair.

For a few moments, he breathed heavily as he heard somebody else enter the room. "Leave us be," the unknown voice said to the men that were trying to scare him. He was thankful that he'd just gotten a reprieve. The mystery man walked up behind him and just stood there for a few seconds. Carl could hear him breathing behind him. Then, he felt the man grab the top of the sandbag and pull it off his head.

At first, the light hurt his eyes. There was a lamp that was shining the light straight at him from only four or five feet away from where he sat. In front of him were a desk and a chair. The room around him had old wallpaper and some broken windows, which explained why he was feeling the cold. Then, he saw the man walk around him and head towards the desk. He remained silent until he was sitting and looking straight back at Carl.

"I want to know your name, your rank, and what army you're with, soldier. You're being accused of spying. Do you know what that means? Let me tell you that the penalty for spying in our country is: death by firing squad!"

Carl didn't attempt to lock eyes with the interrogator. He just stared at the ground and said nothing in response.

"You can stay in that position if you want, but if you're going to waste my time, then I'm going to let the others continue the interrogation. Are you a member of the British Army? Tell me your name," he said as he pulled out a cigarette and lit it with a lighter from his chest pocket.

Babcock was surprised when the man exhaled his smoke and then stood up. He reached into a drawer and pulled out a bottle of soda. He placed it on the desk and opened it. Then he pushed it towards Babcock and said, "You're in our custody now. Not saying anything to me isn't going to work. I need to determine if you're a civilian or if you're a soldier. There are different laws for each one. Have a drink and think about it, hmmm?"

The corporal looked up and stared at the bottle. He then revealed his name, his rank, and his service number, which pleased the interrogator as he started walking behind Corporal Babcock, who grabbed the beverage and took a big swig before putting it back on the desk.

The interrogator didn't say anything for a moment, giving Carl a moment to think about his situation. He kept his gaze at the cement floor. Suddenly, the man was distracted by a knock on the door and went to open it. That was when a different person started speaking to him in another language. The corporal could hear him flicking through paper as he walked back to his desk.

"We already knew that you were a soldier because of your dog tags. The report that we have about the circumstances before your capture was that you were caught with a full pack and rifle with several days of food. So, tell me, Corporal Babcock, what sort of a mission were you on? You were on a classified mission in our country. That puts you in a bad light as far as we're concerned. Who was your unit commander? How can we get in touch with your unit to let them know that you are in custody? Remember that you're not a civilian. You admit that you are a soldier in the British Army. We have no agreements with them anymore. Admit it, you're Special Forces, aren't you? You're a commando."

Carl responded by repeating his name, rank, and serial number to his captor. There was a pause for a few seconds. Then, the interrogator went after him another way. "Are you hungry? Would you like a hot chocolate? It's freezing in here. I'm going to have one. No, seriously. I'm offering you something to warm you up. Something more than this soda. You'll be able to think better. I know how cold it is in the room where we've been keeping you."

Again, Babcock repeated his name, rank, and serial number to the interrogator.

As the man before the desk closed the manila folder, he looked at Carl and offered him something else. "I can get two hot coffees, and I know we have some roast turkey sandwiches in our lunch room. Would you like one? Just tell me what branch of the military you're in, and I'll see to it that you're fed a decent meal. I mean, when is the last time you ate something decent? Those meals they give the commandos don't taste very good, do they?"

Inside his head, Carl was cursing at the man in front of him, who spoke with a Belgian accent. There were a few seconds where nothing more was said between them, and then somebody else in a mask knocked on the door again and brought in two cups of coffee and a sandwich. He put them down on the desk and then left the room.

It all smelled so good as the interrogator put it all in front of him. "You don't want the sandwich? That's too bad. Mind if I have some?"

Carl stopped looking at the sandwich as it was taken away. He listened to the man bite into it and then start chewing theatrically. Knowing that the coffee was real, however, Carl decided to make a move and take the cup that was being offered to him, and he was glad when he did. The corporal took in a big sip. The warmth was life-saving, and he felt his cheeks warm up from the inside out. The warmth gave him a renewed sense of energy.

The interrogator nodded. "Go ahead. Drink it," he repeated. "You like it? I bet it hit the spot. Now, tell me, what were you doing out there? Are you telling me that you were out there in the backcountry just for fun by yourself? Were you alone or was somebody going to resupply you with provisions when you ran out? I wouldn't go out there on my own, you know," the interrogator said as he sat in the chair behind the desk.

Carl said nothing but took in a second sip of the hot coffee. He refused to make eye contact and looked down at the ground when suddenly the interrogator banged the desk causing his cup of coffee to spill and flow over the desk onto Babcock's legs. The pain from the hot liquid was intense and caused him to drop his cup onto the floor.

"I see that you're just wasting my time here, Corporal. I've tried to help you, but you've given me nothing in return. If you don't wish to cooperate, then we can go at this another way, but rest assured, I will get the answers that I seek. Guards, get in here! Take this piece of shit out of my office! He's playing games with me."

Two men then entered the room and put the sandbag over Babcock's head and took him out of the room again. This time, however, they took him into a room that had a broken window, and that made things really cold for him. What they did next, though, truly shocked Carl. One of the guards put him into a stress position that was hard on his legs while the other went to get something from outside of the room. A few seconds later, he found out what it was the guard had gone to get.

There was a radio that was producing loud white static noise and it was quite uncomfortable to have to listen to while still being in a stress position on the floor. But then, things went to another level when a second bucket of water was thrown at Carl's face and upper body. He was soaked right through.

Throughout the night, they were constantly repositioning him and preventing Carl from sleeping. He had muscle cramps, and each time he screamed and fell to the ground. He couldn't get the cramping to stop and this played with his mind severely. He thought again of quitting, but at three in the morning the guards came back into the room and then dragged him out into the hall and into a different room.

Once again they put a sandbag over his head as he was placed into a chair. This time, a woman started asking him questions. He gave the woman a quick response citing his name, rank, and serial number. Then, he stared down but was unable to see anything. Suddenly, two men came up and took him out of the chair and forced him to stand. They took off his clothes and the sandbag.

The woman commented about his penis and thought that he might have a hernia and offered to check for him. She said that she was a doctor. Carl responded with his name, rank and serial number once again.

A few seconds of silence played with his mind. Then the woman pointed at the door and the guards put the sandbag over his head again but this time they didn't allow him to have his clothing. Instead, they dragged him back to the room he'd been taken from, which was quite cold, and now, being naked as he was, the cold was going to cause him to have even more cramping. He didn't know how much longer he could last.

It seemed like every three to four hours, somebody came into the room to get him. Each time, there was a different interrogator, who would try to extract information from him in a different way. There were no more offers of hot coffee or food, though, and these interrogations continued all the way into the evening. While his room was still full of the background static noises of various things such as sirens or babies crying—or just squelching sounds like one would hear on the radio—occasionally, he would hear somebody else having a rough go of it. Babcock would say a prayer and hope that he and whoever was being done over in the other room would somehow find the strength to continue.

By 6 p.m., Carl was a ball of quivering jelly and he was shivering uncontrollably on the floor in the room he had been placed into only recently. The corporal couldn't maintain the position he was put into for more than a few seconds because his legs and calves were cramping all the time, causing him nightmarish pain. He felt like a fish out of water, about to give up on life, when the door to the room he was in opened up. He dreaded being dragged out and questioned again, but this time, it was a man who identified himself as the course medical doctor, who told him that the interrogation phase was now over and that he had passed. Carl thought he was being tricked into revealing something. This guy was trying to fill him with hope and then would walk out of the room when he didn't get the answers that he wanted, and it would devastate him completely.

The doctor looked him over and took the sandbag off of his head so he could see that the physical was going to stay with him for a while until Babcock could accept that he'd just made it through the final phase of the selection course.

The man had a very tough time convincing Carl that the course was over and that he'd actually made it through the final phase of it. Eventually, however, Carl came to his senses and started crying while the doctor had the background noises stopped. When the sounds stopped, that was the moment when Babcock trusted his inner voice that told him he'd made it through selection.

The work that Carl had done to get through all the phases was indescribable. It had tested every ounce of faith that he had in his personal abilities. His past experiences had helped him, but this course had definitely tested his mettle. He'd had to dig deep on this one, but he was thankful that he'd already proven out on the open ocean and in Papua New Guinea that he could find his own way to survive challenging times. He also knew that if his father were there right now, he'd be smiling from ear to ear that his son had done the impossible.

Graciously, the physician allowed Carl all the time he needed to come back to reality, and when he was ready, the doctor helped him stand up and walk out of the room. He was taken to a warmer room, given clean clothes and a hot meal, and then he and a few other men were taken by truck to a base, where they were put into their own rooms for the night.

The next morning, shortly after breakfast, the six men that had made it to the end were marched into the office of the course officer by Sergeant Mitchell. It was Lieutenant Colonel Plante who gave them their congratulations and a handshake. Then, he gave each one of them a beret with the winged dagger hat badge on it. After the informal ceremony, he gave them all a bit of advice too. "There is no time for egos to get swollen. The training continues, and you can be kicked out of my unit at the snap of my fingers. There are missions that we must perform very soon, and we are to get you ready for those. Now get out of my office and wait in the hall," he said firmly but politely.

While they waited for Sergeant Mitchell to come and collect them, the six men chatted amongst themselves, enjoying the moment. Out of forty-two men, only six had made it to graduation. The feeling of euphoria that they all felt was going to stick with them for the rest of their lives.

Chapter 2

Captain Kurt Sommer—a commercial fisherman whose boat was now en route to an area of the German coastline gazed at his wristwatch. It read 2 a.m. He hadn't slept very much and had already vomited up the small meal that he'd ingested the previous evening due to some really bad weather that was making his boat, the *Blue Gem*, move in all sorts of directions that his body didn't like very much.

While he repositioned himself in his bunk space, which was situated in a small room on board his commercial fishing boat, Kurt hoped that most of his projectile vomit would find the bucket that he'd put on the floor beside his bunk before he'd lain down, but it was dark and he wasn't sure what kind of mess was now on the floor beneath him.

They'd been at sea now for well over forty-eight hours and neither he nor his first mate, Derek Lang, had slept very much. They needed to make up for lost time due to engine problems that had kept them tied up on the dock. British Intelligence had sent them out to sea to observe and to report any observations that they saw near the German/Netherlands Coastline, and they were still miles from their objective.

The captain of the *Blue Gem* hoped that his first mate Derek Lang would be able to handle the boat during these rough conditions while he rested. Mother Nature had decided to put them through a pretty heavy storm front, which was making their travel on the seas quite harsh. As a result of the waves, Kurt couldn't sleep a wink, try as he might, and the nausea was starting to hit him hard. He was nervous too because they happened to be aboard a ship in the middle of a turbulent ocean while in the complete darkness of the night off of Germany's coastline, which was heavily patrolled by enemy ships. As he pondered what might be in store for them, he was tipped out of his bunk and thrown onto the floor as a rogue wave struck the side of the vessel.

Sprawled out on the floor, Kurt discovered that he'd missed the bucket at least once as his beard and chest moved through the smelly contents that he'd landed in. Slowly, he managed to get up onto one knee and then reached for the bunk with one of his hands. The captain then stood back up and started removing his soiled clothes while trying to keep his balance.

After his clothes were off, he washed his face, using the washbasin that he filled up with water on his small table in his quarters. His beard was emitting a foul smell, and he wanted to be clean before he got into new clothes.

Ten minutes later, he was dressed in a clean shirt, underwear, and pants again, but before he went topside to see if his Derek needed help, he sat down on a chair and put on a pair of socks that he took out from a drawer that was under his bunk. While he was putting on his second wool sock, another wave hit the boat. "Shit!" He swore out loud as he reached for the side of the bed to stable himself. A moment later, his vessel rolled to one side and then rolled back the other way. When the boat steadied itself, Kurt put on his shoes and did them up fast before another wave could hit.

Upstairs in the wheelhouse, Derek was trying to navigate the boat in the direction that he'd been ordered to go. While trying to remain positive, he watched the many dark clouds cover the stars as they approached their boat. Looking out the main window in the wheelhouse, he could see the waves rolling around in front of him. They were getting pretty big, which was a real concern because the engine had been acting up on the previous fishing trip, and they hadn't done a full engine rebuild, which was what it needed, being as old as it was.

Derek wondered if the captain was feeling any better, but he had his doubts that he'd be getting any sleep down in his quarters due to the rocking of the vessel. What if the engine failed on them out there? If it died in this horrendous weather, there would be no one coming to their rescue. The first mate kept his hands on the wheel and looked at the boat's compass. He was still going in the right direction, but he saw no land in sight and came to the conclusion that they were behind schedule.

Looking over at a map that was pinned up on the wall of the wheelhouse, Derek rechecked his heading and tried to calculate how much farther they would have to go before they hit the German coastline that was close to the Netherlands. That required some measurements and some math, so he put the boat on automatic drive and walked over to the map and stared at it closely for several minutes until he thought he had his route figured out. Then, he sat at a small table and started doing calculations. He had been deep in thought for at least ten minutes when he was distracted by the sounds of many planes flying high above the boat.

The first mate walked towards the door that took him outside onto the main deck and opened it. He was immediately hit with rain and surrounded by very loud engine sounds that belonged to dozens of planes that he couldn't see. He was going in the right direction all right. The bombers were British, and they were on their way to the German coastline too. It sounded like the first wave of Bombers that they had been told to watch out for.

As Lang tried to determine how many planes were flying above their fishing vessel, he walked carefully down to the door that went down to the galley, engine room, and personal quarters. He went down the stairs, holding on to the side rail as he descended the steps, and was soon at the captain's door, which he knocked on hard. "Captain, the bombers are flying over us right now! Come on out here and see them for yourself," he said. Suddenly, the door opened and Kurt Sommer walked out of his room. He looked at his first mate and replied, "I was coming up anyway. Let's go and see what's happening out there, Derek!"

When they both got topside, the planes were still flying over them, but they couldn't see any of them because the clouds were obstructing their view. "How many do you think there are, Captain?" Derek asked as he looked up into the sky as his face was hit with rain.

Sommer was amazed by the loudness of the engines. "I can hardly say. They're so many of them. It'd be hard to say exactly how many there are, but they're on track for the mission," he answered as they walked carefully back to the wheelhouse, holding on to rails that surrounded the top deck of the ship.

They'd obviously had some good luck so far from what they could deduce. Nobody had attacked them yet, and perhaps this storm was helping them avoid detection, Kurt thought as he took over the wheel and checked his compass bearing. He then took the automatic drive off and sped up. Their boat should have been many miles from where they were by now, and he knew that he needed to hurry up because the mission wasn't going to wait for them to reach the position that they were supposed to be at by 3 a.m.

When he was sure that the boat was going ahead as fast as it could—in the proper direction—he looked over to his first mate, who was watching the waves that were coming straight at them through the main window. "This is bad weather, Derek! Have you checked all the hatches on the main deck since last night?" The first mate shook his head. "Not since 6 p.m. sir. We were busy worrying about the engine, remember?"

Sommer grunted and walked by his first mate. He put on his jacket that was on the coat rack by the back of the door and then said, "You take the wheel. I'm going to make bloody sure that we don't sink," the captain replied, but just as Kurt finished speaking, the bow was hit by a giant wave, which sent ocean spray in every direction, and they were unable to see anything through the windows of the wheelhouse. A few moments later, they could see through them again, so the captain walked over to the door and opened it. "I'll be checking the front and rear hatches. I hope to be back within twenty minutes," Kurt said to Derek as he left through the open door. The sounds of the bombers still could be heard as they flew ahead of them.

The first mate looked at his captain and nodded as he watched him walk out into the pouring rain. "Okay, I'll try and keep the boat steady while you do that. I'm coming to find you if you're not back here in fifteen minutes, sir," he replied, but Kurt couldn't hear him with all the sounds going on outside all around him.

As Derek put the boat on autopilot, he looked at the compass once more to ensure that they were heading in the right direction. At least they could report that the bombers were well on their way to their target, but they were under orders of sticking to radio silence until after the attack had commenced. That being said, it would be quite hard to report back to British Intelligence with any kind of accurate information with this storm raging all around them as it was.

While Lang stared through the main window of the wheelhouse, he knew that they had to focus on keeping themselves alive first and foremost. The main concern was the engine. It couldn't be pushed too hard, and yet, that was exactly what they were doing at that particular moment in time. How they would ever see German U-boats in these kinds of waves was beyond Lang's reasoning, but they'd been told to report any sightings of German Navy Vessels, U-boats, or British submarines to the British Intelligence if they observed them.

Meanwhile, Captain Sommer was making sure that the hatch in front of the boat was securely fastened. When he was satisfied that it was tied down properly, he looked up to the sky. He could still hear the roar of multiple bombers, but he couldn't see any of them. The only thing he could see was the flock of white seagulls that were flying above the boat, and he wondered why they were out there over such rough seas.

Kurt looked up at the birds after he was done with the hatch on the bow. "Good question, Mr Bird. A bloody good question!" he said, smiling, and then walked to the back of the boat to check on the hatch, then the engine and the exhaust systems, which required him to go back down into the boat to check.

When he got to the stern, he saw that it was tied down but the waves had loosened up the ropes. Quickly, he undid some of them and retied them. Suddenly, a wave hit the side of the boat, and he was knocked sideways. Kurt grabbed onto one of the ropes that he had been securing to the hatch and held on tight as the vessel rolled one way and then returned to its full upright position. When he was sure that he'd be okay standing back up, he made his move and got onto one knee again as he finished securing the hatch.

A few moments later, the captain walked away from the rear hatch and headed over to the door that took him inside the bowels of the boat. As the boat rocked from yet another wave hitting its side, Kurt put out both of his arms so that he wouldn't fall. It wasn't easy descending the stairs while the boat was being tossed first to the left and then to the right, but he moved one hand to a side rail and managed not to fall down or break any bones.

When the captain got down the staircase, he walked past the galley and his quarters. He continued to another door that took him down yet another set of stairs, which led to the engine room. When he got there, he immediately put on some ear protection and then walked into the main engine room, which was making a great deal of noise. Sommer didn't see anything out of the ordinary, which was a good sign. He walked over to some pressure gauges, looked at those, and then decided to test the oil level in the engine. Normally, the engine had to be off when doing an oil level check, but he didn't dare turn it off now. His measurement wouldn't be perfectly accurate, but he could get a general idea if it was full or empty, and after he had a look at the dipstick, he discovered that it was pretty low and was now very glad that he had checked it.

Twenty minutes later, the Captain entered the wheelhouse, looking like a drowned rat. He released a heavy sigh and was thankful to be out of the rain. Still, the boat was moving from side to side, up and down, as it climbed over the giant waves. Both men were feeling ill, but it wasn't incapacitating them to the point that they couldn't perform their duties.

Derek looked at Kurt and smiled at him. "How did things go, Captain? Did you hear the bombers out there? I think I just heard a second wave of them heading in the same direction as the first. How many waves are they going to send do you think? That's a lot of planes heading over to Germany! They must really want to destroy something pretty badly I reckon."

The captain nodded and grunted as he took a towel that was hanging on the coat rack. He dried off his face and then took the towel to his head. As he removed his jacket a short time later, he replied, "The German fighters should be on the first wave shortly, but this storm front has shielded the British, so they're quite lucky that they weren't attacked on the way in. I hope they get to their objective and make a whole lot of damage because I don't want to be out here in this shitty weather for nothing!"

"You can say that again." the first mate replied as he looked out the main window of the old wheelhouse. He looked over in the captain's direction and saw his face. It wasn't pink as usual. Instead, it looked ashen grey as the captain began to reply. "I would suggest that we shouldn't be pushing the engine so . . ." Suddenly a wave of nausea fell over the captain, and he stopped speaking for a second as he tried to keep himself from vomiting, but he couldn't hold it down and soon spewed all over the wheelhouse floor.

He quickly left the wheelhouse, went outside onto the main deck, and then stumbled over to the side of the ship. When his hands met the rails, he vomited up green bile and sent it overboard while the sea spray crashed up and into his face. The salt water stung his eyes as the tears streamed down his cheeks. Kurt wiped his mouth off on his sleeve as he watched the waves rise and fall around his boat. His head was spinning, and he felt faint. Derek called out to him as he stood at the doorway quite concerned for Sommer's safety. Off in the distance, he could see the waves churning and rolling towards their ship. It wasn't a good time to be outside, so he yelled out and warned Kurt to hold on to the rails firmly.

"Hold on, Captain. I'm putting the boat on automatic. Just a second," he said and then ran back inside the wheelhouse. A few moments went by, and then the first mate was outside on his way to help Kurt as yet another wave crashed into the bow of the boat, causing an explosion of sea spray to shoot off in every direction.

When he got to Sommer, he asked him if he was alright, but before he could hear a reply from him, they were both hit by a large volume of water that took them off of their feet and flattened them on the deck, soaking them completely. But neither one went over the rails, thankfully. "Captain, come inside. Come inside! We can't be out here in this," the first mate shouted as he attempted to help his boss get back to the wheelhouse.

It took a few moments for the two men to recover from the frigid waters that had soaked them to the bone. "Come on, Captain. It's now or never. Let's get back inside," Lang said as he got onto one knee and helped Kurt get up off of the deck.

More waves hit the boat, throwing them both off-balance, but they managed to stumble back towards the wheelhouse. They had to take it slowly, one foot at a time, as they helped each other get back, but soon they found their way back to the door. When they felt they were out of danger, they shook their heads at each other, acknowledging the state they were now in—completely soaked and freezing cold. They managed to smile at each other now that they knew they'd survived that scary moment out on deck.

When they got inside, the first mate pulled out a chair for the captain to sit on and put a metal bucket beside him. Then, he passed him the towel, which Captain Sommer accepted with thanks. Derek then walked back to the steering wheel and took the boat off of its automatic drive again while waves crashed against the bow of the boat and obscured his direct view in front of the vessel as it chugged along heading towards their objective.

Lang took off the soaking-wet wool sweater that his wife had given to him and threw it in the corner. Then, he went over to a wooden box that was beside the steering wheel and opened it up. Inside was an emergency pack that he had prepared in case he needed to go to shore, and it had many provisions that he'd placed in the main compartment, including some dry clothes and a wool blanket.

"I have some ginger in the first aid pouch. I'll get it for you," Derek said as he undid his shoes and pulled them off. He took off his socks as Kurt suddenly tried to vomit again, but there was nothing coming up, so he was now dry heaving, which Lang knew hurt the guts tremendously. The captain then replied with an "okay" before reaching for the sick bucket and dry-retching one more time.

After Derek had changed his clothes and put his feet into a new pair of socks, he stepped into the rain boots that they kept in the wheelhouse. They were warm, and he felt much better, but when he looked over at Kurt, he saw a very sick man sitting down on the chair. Remembering the first aid kit, he went back into his pack and pulled it out. He walked over to his captain and said, "We need to get you out of those wet clothes. I have some pants and a shirt in my pack for you, but first, bite off a piece of this ginger root and start chewing on it. It'll stop the vomiting. We have to deal with that first," he said as he started to untie Kurt's shoes.

After drying off Sommer with the towel, Derek thought about what he wanted to say next. "We're going to have to send out a message as soon as the bombing begins. We need you to stay up here and man the wheelhouse while I go downstairs and reassemble the transmitter.

Kurt began nodding. "I'll be fine. I know this will work. We still have some time."

At 3 a.m., Captain Sommer was manning the steering wheel in the wheelhouse when he was suddenly distracted by multiple red lights that were seen quite a ways inland between Germany and the Netherlands, which his boat was finally approaching. There were so many explosions that Kurt wanted to go out onto the main deck and look through his telescope. First, though, he put his boat on automatic drive and reached for the spyglass that he had in the corner behind the coat rack.

As he looked towards the German coastline from outside on the deck, he could see multiple fiery explosions going off way back in the German mountains. There was also a raging forest fire, and he could also hear a third wave of bombers heading towards the same area. Clearly, the bombers had reached their destination as the red fiery lights reflected against the clouds that were high above the target. Those pilots were still able to drop their payloads, and he hoped that they were destroying whatever they were hitting as he put his coat back on and went to find his first mate and tell him to send another message to British Intelligence.

As he walked over to the doorway that was on the side of the fishing vessel, he looked at the German coastline and then up towards the many clouds that were miles inland. The light from the explosions looked like an angry ripple of red light as each explosion sent a new wave of light across a multitude of clouds hanging above the mountains where they were dropping their bombs.

When he reached the door to the stairway that led him down into the galley and the other compartments of the boat, he quickly opened the door and carefully descended the staircase. He didn't have to walk very far because there was Derek working on the radio on the galley table.

When Kurt approached him, he was busy listening to the radio receiver and jotting down a message. The first mate looked up as the boat leaned starboard due to an impacting wave. The storm had not forgotten about them. He refocused and started writing down the Morse code message while Captain Sommer waited patiently. He was feeling more stable now that he had ingested several pieces of ginger. Kurt could see that his first mate was going to be busy for a few minutes, so he wrote down a message and put it beside him. Lang immediately gave him the thumbs up.

Sommer nodded his head as he chewed on some ginger. "To right, mate. Go on then. Send the message when you're done. I'll head back topside," he said as he went back into the hallway and started climbing the stairs again. He didn't like being away from the wheelhouse in such a serious storm and wanted to get back to it as soon as possible.

When Captain Sommer got topside, he saw more red flashes impacting the same target area his boat continued to approach. He wondered what had been there and expected that whatever was there was now heavily damaged. The first wave of bombers had reached their objective. There was no doubt about that, but where was the German's response? Surely they would be retaliating, he thought, as he walked along the main deck, heading towards the wheelhouse.

As the boat continued moving through the rough seas, another rogue wave suddenly hit the deck and took out Kurt's legs, nearly washing him overboard. This time, it was up to him to save himself because Derek was below and had no idea that his captain had almost been washed overboard.

Kurt had the experience to look for the base of the rails, and as he was washed down the deck, he wrapped both of his arms around the first solid piece of metal he could see. This saved his life, as the water ran past him and spilt out over the deck into the angry ocean. He looked up and saw the wheelhouse, and above it flew several more seagulls that were coasting in the wind, watching him like he was in some kind of play.

"I'm not going to die tonight," he said as he waited until all the water was off the deck. Then, he crawled away from the railing and moved slowly towards the door of the wheelhouse. He managed to get to the wall, found a safety line, and pulled himself up with it. A few moments later, he put his hand on the doorknob and turned it until the door opened and he was able to walk back inside the wheelhouse again.

Below deck, the first mate was concentrating as he sent out a message to a British submarine that was supposed to be patrolling in the area and supporting them with communications or anything else they could proffer. Lang was now transmitting the message that the captain had just brought down, and he knew that the commander of the submarine would be quite happy to learn that bombs were now landing on target—and that, so far, no German response had been seen.

When he finished a few minutes later, he listened for a reply and soon heard the Morse code signals coming back to him. His concentration was laser-sharp. It was one thing to hear the bleeps and the pauses in a classroom, but being out at sea in the middle of a crazy storm on the German coast made things much more stressful.

When he heard nothing further after another minute of focused concentration, he took off his earphones and tried to stretch and ease up his sore lower back. Then, he took apart the transmitter and started putting it all back into its secret hiding spot in case the boat should be boarded by the German navy and searched.

Meanwhile, below the surface of the stormy seas near the German coastline, a British submarine known as the *HMS Seadog* was coasting at periscope depths with all engines off, remaining as silent as possible. "Sir, I have multiple messages from the fishing trawler using the new coding system," said Corporal Owens, the radio operator for that current shift.

Commander Hayes acknowledged him and asked him what the message said as he watched the corporal work away at deciphering the message. "Mission Grapefruit has begun, sir. The second message says that the first load of fish has been delivered. That's all it says," reported the corporal as the commander paced around the con. He then scratched his unshaven face and gave another order to the corporal.

"Send a message to London. Tell them we have confirmation that the first wave of bombers has dropped its payload and has been met with little resistance thus far."

"Yes, sir," Owens said as he started working on a message back at his station. Commander Hayes went over to his navigator and asked him for their exact position. The blonde-haired Lieutenant looked at the chart that was on a table near him and started working on figuring out exactly where they were. A few moments later, Lieutenant Conroy pointed to an area near the German coastline. "We're here, sir."

Commander Hayes walked over to the map and looked inland off of Germany's coast. He saw the mountain that held the underground base underneath it but he doubted that the bombs would have any effect on a base that was estimated to be several hundred feet underground. As he looked at the map and saw his location in relation to the fishing trawler's, he hoped he was wrong, but all he thought this mission would accomplish would be to let the Germans know that the allies were aware of their secret base. He kept his negativity to himself, though, as he thanked his navigational officer and called one of his petty officers over to him.

Petty Officer Barber walked over to him and was given the order to go down to the engine room and pass on a message that the Commander wanted to know if the fuel problem was fixed yet. They had been having problems with one of their engines and its fuel pump. It had been a problem for the past six hours, and he wanted to know what in the hell was taking them so long to fix it. "Tell them not to drop anything. Metal on metal can be heard for hundreds of meters underwater. But make sure they're careful," said Hayes.

The Petty officer looked directly at his commanding officer and said, "Yes sir," and then turned around and went off to get an update, trying very hard not to make any additional noise as he moved through the open hatch door that sectioned off the compartment from the next one.

Chapter 3

At the same time that the bombing raid was taking place somewhere in the mountains of Germany, the Commanding Officer of the 5th SAS Regiment, Lieutenant Colonel Gaston Plante paddled in his folboat alongside seven other members of his unit. They had paddled up to the German coastline from the Netherlands, but due to rough seas, they had not been able to make it to shore and it was an amazing feat that they were still alive due to the savageness of the ocean storm surrounding them.

Under the cover of darkness, the group headed towards their objective while the bombers from the second wave of attacks continued to fly out to sea. The ocean was not cooperating with the men in their small collapsible boats. Already, several of his men had capsized due to waves hitting them and turning them over. Nobody had been lost yet, but they were being slowed down considerably, as they had to rescue those who had capsized.

The mountains off in the distance were also cloaked in darkness. Plante was expecting German fighters to engage the bombers momentarily as the allied bombers left the safety of the mountains. He watched the skies carefully as the roar of the bomber engines sounded over them. They could all see the red fiery glow deep within the countryside of their enemy and believed that extensive damage had been done.

By half-past three in the morning, the ocean was starting to ease up and the clouds were starting to dissipate, but by no means was the storm over. Plante couldn't shake the bad feeling he had, and he felt like a bundle of nerves. This feeling was proven to be correct when suddenly dozens of balls of light shot out of the mountains and headed towards the bombers, illuminating the dark skies.

They left fizzling, pale lines of light in their wake. The commander could see the tracer rounds from the bombers firing back at the glowing orbs of light when several fighters showed up to engage the allied bombers. Suddenly, they decided to change direction and head back into the mountains, having concluded that a third wave of bombers was laying siege to the side of the mountain where the underground base was known to be.

Plante saw the balls of light cause several of the retreating bombers to crash into other planes and fall down to the ocean not too far away from where they were. After several of the second wave bombers went down, the balls of light joined the German fighters, which then went back over the mountains as bombs continued to explode on the mountainous countryside quite a distance away from where they were situated.

Plante couldn't believe what he and the other commandos had been witness to. There were dozens of balls of light flying at unbelievable speeds and angles that no human being could survive due to the G-forces that were involved. He wondered what they could possibly be.

One of the bomber's pilots on the third wave, Captain Will Fairleigh, was soon blinded by one of the balls of light that had caught up to his aircraft. It seemed to be flying around the plane somehow. "What the Hell is that thing?" he yelled to his co-pilot. "It's making it impossible for me to see the other planes!"

"Sweet Mother Mary! Close one of your eyes so you can keep your night vision," replied Lieutenant Williams, the co-pilot of the plane. The navigational officer looked out the side window and watched as the glowing lights darted between the bombers to try and prevent them from successfully dropping their bombs on target. "What the hell are those things, Captain?"

The senior pilot was able to see several bombers that were in front of their aircraft and steered the plane to their immediate right so as to avoid flying into them. "I haven't got a clue, but whatever they are, they're trying to prevent us from getting on target. Navigational officer, check with the bombardier. See if he's okay."

The navigational officer undid his safety belt and went to check on the bombardier, who seemed to be focused on dropping their payload. Lieutenant Cummings watched him as he looked through an aiming site and decided not to disturb him for the moment. He waited for several seconds and then spoke. "Captain wants to know if you're having any problems. Are you still on target?"

The bombardier looked up and nodded his head. "There's something else out there, sir. Can you guys see them? They're trying to stop us from dropping our bombs, whatever they are. Bloody foo fighters! I got no other name for them. They're balls of light. What are they? Do you know?" Sergeant Gregorchuck asked.

Cummings shook his head as he watched one of the machine gunners start firing his weapon at one of the balls of light. It got out of the way of the rounds being fired at it in an instant. "I have no idea what they are. Captain wants to know if he needs to turn around so you can have another crack at it?"

Gregorchuck shook his head and then looked back into the bombing site. "No. I'm dropping the bombs now. Counting down. Three. Two. One. Bombs away!" He then pressed a button and dozens of bombs that were in the bomb bay were released, dropping towards their intended target.

Cummings went back to his seat and put on his headset. He spoke through it and reported that their bombs had been dropped on target. Captain Fairleigh nodded his head in acknowledgement as he tried to get away from another plane that was getting too close to them. Several machine gunners on other planes were firing at the flying balls of light, but they were forgetting that there were other planes that their bullets would hit if they weren't careful.

The skies were full of red tracers, which made flying their bomber extremely difficult. Fairleigh shut one of his eyes, hoping that this would prevent any blindness. One of the foo fighters, as Gregorchuck had started calling them, was getting too close to their cockpit and it seemed like the senior pilot was flying their aircraft into the sun itself. The light was so intense that both the pilot and the co-pilot could see the brightness in front of them even if they shut their eyes.

As Captain Fairleigh did his best to avoid the balls of light, two of the bombers that were in front of him started firing at them. He watched in horror as one of the planes hit the wing of the other one and suddenly erupted into flames after the rounds from their machine guns ruptured the fuel tanks. Suddenly, the ship exploded, leaving no chance for survival.

There was nothing that Williams and his captain could do but to take evasive action and avoid any of the debris, which was easier said than done. A split second later, their bomber was pasted with metal fragments and they lost their communication system entirely.

To make matters worse, their read gunner started firing at the balls of light that he saw above their plane. The red tracers lit up the sky as they came close to several of the unidentified lights. The captain got on his mic and started yelling at them. "Check your fire. Check your fire! Your rounds are coming close to the other bombers! Remember, we have our own aircraft out there! Do you guys hear me? Acknowledge!"

But there was no answer.

Fairleigh looked over at his co-pilot and said, "I need you to go back there and see what's going on. I've lost comms."

Lieutenant Williams immediately undid his safety belt and went to see what was going on. As he walked by the navigator, he asked him to check his headset. "Do you have comms? We're not hearing anyone. Check amongst yourselves. I'll go back to the rear and see if they can hear us."

Cummings started doing radio checks and soon discovered that he couldn't hear anyone. He got up out of his seat and went to the front of the plane where he saw Captain Fairleigh. "Sir, I think the system is down. I can't hear anyone on our internal system."

The captain nodded. "Thanks for telling me. We must have taken a hit from the planes in front of us. We need to get out of here fast," he replied.

At the back of the plane, Lieutenant Williams was ordering the rear gunner to stop firing his guns. When he stopped, the young airman looked at the co-pilot and wondered why he wasn't in the cockpit. He took off his headset and listened to what the Lieutenant was screaming at him.

"Corporal Johnson! We've lost communications. Stop firing your guns at those things. The tracers are hitting other planes. We just lost two planes in front of us. Watch the other aircraft around us before you fire them again. Don't hit their wings! I'm heading back to the cockpit. Can you hear us talking to you?"

The gunner shook his head and said, "No, sir. Can't hear you."

Williams looked back at him and said, "You and Sergeant Haley have to communicate with each other, okay? Keep an eye on him. We can't hear you either. You need to do hand signals from here on out, okay?"

Williams got a thumbs up from the young airman and then turned and walked back to Haley, who was the senior gunner. He spoke to him quickly and told him that communications were down and that hand signals between him and the other machine gunner were essential. When the co-pilot was satisfied that he understood what he was saying to him, he slapped him on the back and continued forwards.

Williams buckled back into his seat and reported to his captain. "Sir, the comms are down all the way to the back of the plane. They're doing hand signals with each other," he reported. The captain nodded and pointed to the right of the plane. There, they could both see another bomber being harassed by a foo fighter. They seemed to be trying to make it hard for the bombers to escape. They moved as though they were living things.

Williams shook his head in disbelief as another ball of light zipped by their window right in front of them. "This is unbelievable," he said. "What are those things?"

Corporal Johnson began shooting at the light as it ducked around the back of their aircraft and looked as if it was about to attack them. "Hold still, you damned thing!" Corporal Johnson shouted.

Suddenly, their bomber was ripped apart by rounds fired from a German fighter, and the gunner near Gregorchuck was ripped to pieces and fell to the floor. The bombardier moved over to him to check on his condition and soon discovered that he was dead. He had to go to the cockpit and tell Captain Fairleigh that Sergeant Haley had been killed.

The German fighter wasn't finished with them yet, though. It dove down towards them firing all of its guns on a second run at them. The gunner at the back started firing at the enemy fighter, but the pilot of the German plane had them in his sites and started firing at a rapid rate. The rounds that he fired were on target as they ripped through the wings and the engines of Fairleigh's bomber, causing the engines to sputter and then fail completely.

As a result, they fell from formation and lost altitude quickly. As the captain attempted to regain control of his plane, he could see that two of his engines were shooting flames out over the wings as he glanced out through the side window of the cockpit. It would only be a minute or so before the plane blew up. He looked over at his co-pilot and gave the order. "Bail out, Williams. Bail out! Get everyone out of here now!"

Lieutenant Williams looked at his captain for a second and quickly processed what was happening as more of the glowing orbs of light shot past their windows and Nazi fighters engaged several bombers as they attacked each one from above. The situation seemed dire. Williams nodded his head and undid his seatbelt. "I'll tell the rest of the crew."

The G-forces made it almost impossible to rise out of the chair though as the plane started to nosedive. Suddenly a wing broke off on the captain's side of the bomber. A bright light lit up the darkness around them outside their aircraft. It was the end of the line for the crew aboard Fairleigh's bomber as the fuel ignited.

The pilots and the crew went down with the plane, unable to get out in time, and the plane dove away from the others that were still flying. A few minutes later, a fiery explosion lit up part of the mountainside that had previously been covered in darkness.

Down on the ocean, the commanding officer of the Belgium Special Air Service looked into the mountains in front of him as the sky filled up with another fiery explosion. They were too far away to know what had happened, but Plante felt sorry for the next wave of bombers that was coming in to drop their bombs. The Germans were now ready to repel them with all the weapons that they had available to them. There would be a huge loss of life; of this, he had no doubt.

Plante couldn't worry about the bombers anymore, however. He had more immediate concerns as he and several others paddled towards one of their own that had been capsized and needed recovery. Corporal Babcock had managed to get to the man who was fighting to stay afloat, and he held onto his folboat as rough seas tried to separate him from his small collapsible boat.

As Carl came alongside him, he told the soaking wet soldier that he was there. "Don't worry, mate. I see you. Hang on," he shouted at his friend. The highly trained soldier that was trying to keep his head above the water heard him, and even though he was freezing and soaked to the skin, he didn't give up on solving his problems as he tried to figure out how to get his boat right-side-up as soon as Babcock got in a position where he could help him.

As the commanding officer watched Babcock help the soldier who was in the water, he knew that they had to get to shore quickly. It wasn't far away, but he knew the sea would soon be full of German Navy.

By the time they got back underway, it was close to four in the morning. Soon, they would lose their cover of darkness and be exposed if they were still out on the open sea. The coastline was very close, and the commanding officer needed to push everyone to get over to it as soon as possible so they could land and hide their boats.

Plante could only hope that the Royal Marine commandos who had been added to the mission would be where they were supposed to meet them as he looked back at everyone behind his boat to make sure that they were all there. Hopefully, the Royal Marines hadn't had such a difficult landing because they were being dropped off by a British submarine and were there to offer the 5th SAS additional support while they headed towards the location of the underground base, which was quite far away from where they would land on the coastline. Plante wasn't sure how many days and nights it would take to reach their objective, but he knew it would take quite a while.

Inside the mountain in Germany, where the secret manufacturing and research facility existed, the commander of the base, General Peter Matz, was handing an SS officer, who was dressed in a black uniform, several manila folders and folded schematic drawings so he could put them into a briefcase. "We're leaving now," the SS captain said. Please order your men up to the secret landing strip and clear it so I can make my escape, General. Where are these scientists I need to take with me?" asked Captain Vunderbane as he put the folders and the drawings into his briefcase, which he then attached to his wrist with a pair of handcuffs.

The General ordered his intelligence officer, Captain Wilhelm Otter, to go and see what was holding them up. Then, Captain Vunderbane replied by saying, "These two scientists understand the complexities of this project, General. We've had problems with the developments we made in the previous year, and if they truly have found the solutions to those problems, then Himmler wants to know about it right away."

The two men continued to talk for several minutes until the Intelligence officer returned with the two scientists as sirens continued to go off everywhere underground in every tunnel and every room. The noise was mind-numbing, and it angered the SS captain considerably. "Can we shut those things off? We know we're being attacked. Who doesn't feel those concussion waves from the bombs they're dropping?"

The commander of the underground base gave out orders to shut off some of the alarms at their present location. Immediately, the intelligence officer working for General Matz left the room and issued several commands to terminate the alarms so that they could focus on figuring what to do next without such loud noises distracting them.

When the alarms stopped, Vunderbane reminded the general that the Fuehrer wanted copies of all the plans that were about the current research being conducted there at the facility. "Make sure everyone gets to the castle safely captain. It will not be easy flying with all of those bombers flying around," the general commented as he handed the SS Captain a cylindrical container, which was used to protect important drawings. "I expected that you would ask me for such things, and I had them prepared for you. It's all in there," the general replied.

Suddenly, vibrations were shaking the floors as bombs landed 450 feet above them. Parts of the concrete cracked, and pieces fell off of the walls from the ceiling. The general took a look around and realized that the bombing was having an effect on the underground tunnels. "They've found us. I have no more time to stay, General. Himmler's orders to you are to ensure that the tunnels are not breached. I suggest you set up defensive forces underground at every level so that enemy forces do not get very far inside, should they try to find their way in here. They obviously know that we are here, but remember: that they must not find out about the lower levels. Have I made Himmler's orders perfectly clear to you, General?"

General Matz nodded, "perfectly clear, Captain."

After replying to the SS officer, he waved his intelligence officer back into the room and gave him more orders. "Escort Captain Vunderbane to the airstrip right away, Captain Otter. His plane must take off immediately without being seen!"

The SS officer gathered his things and then looked at the General one last time. "Heil Hitler," Captain Vunderbane said to the base commander. "Good luck," the General replied as he raised his arm to return the salute.

The General's intelligence officer immediately responded by nodding and immediately ordered several guards to come with him as he escorted the SS officer out of the meeting room and into a main tunnel. They walked for a fair distance, revealing how long the tunnels actually were, but had to stop and brace themselves as the rock walls shook from the concussion waves caused by the bombing that was still going on above.

Coming towards them, there were many soldiers marching in groups of fifteen men. They assumed their defensive positions underground while Captain Otter continued to lead the SS officer to the escape tunnel that led out to the airstrip. As Vunderbane walked onwards, and he noticed the Nazi eagle painted over a smoothed out section on one of the walls. Below it was a marker of the number six tunnel—escape access with an arrow that pointed down another tunnel that they were about to reach.

The lights suddenly began to short-circuit, and for a second, they were immersed in darkness. Then, they came back to life, and once again, Captain Otter resumed walking towards the escape hatch. A few moments later, more German soldiers ran past them as they headed back in the direction of the general, but now there was an incline as they walked uphill for nine hundred yards until they came to a flat level marking the end of their underground journey.

At the end of the tunnel was a spiral staircase, which led upwards by at least thirty feet to a hatch. When the SS officer reached the top of the stairs, he looked at the Nazi marker next to the secret entrance to the tunnels in the ceiling and could see that it was the right place to exit from, as it had "airstrip access" written in German below the Nazi eagle insignia. Vunderbane opened the hatch and breathed in the cold night's air.

After listening for a few seconds, he poked his head outside of the fake tree stump that was hidden out in the forest. Captain Vunderbane could hear the bombers flying over the mountains nearby and smelled the smoke from the forest fires that were burning in the valley where they now were. As he looked around, he too could see the white balls of light zooming around the retreating bombers. That made him smile, but he said nothing to alert the scientists who were following closely behind him. His eyes glimmered from the reflection of the flames higher up on another mountainside as he crawled out of the fake stump and allowed the two scientists, Hilda Richter and Henry Newmann, to follow him out of the secret entrance.

When they were all on the surface, they soon saw more explosions hammering the mountain where the hidden base was located underground. Another German officer saw them from his camouflaged trench and quickly left his hiding space beneath some camouflage netting to go over to get them at the fake tree stump that the SS officer had climbed out of. He greeted the SS officer and escorted them over to a plane that was getting ready to leave.

The darkness was starting to lessen as dawn announced itself, and the smell of burning wood was intense for everyone—as was the amount of smoke, which made it hard to breathe. The scientists quickly pulled out handkerchiefs and covered their noses and mouths so they could breathe in decent air.

When they reached the plane, the pilot was checking the wings and making sure it was ready to go. It wasn't a big plane, but it could hold several passengers. When the pilot saw them coming towards him, he waved them forward and helped them get into the aircraft.

The pilot reported to the SS officer and took his new orders to heart. Then, he made sure the runway was clear for takeoff while the SS Captain ushered his scientists to buckle up and expect a rough take-off. "Hurry now," said the SS officer to the scientists. He made sure both Dr Newmann and Dr Richtman were onboard before getting in himself.

While Captain Vunderbane buckled into his co-pilot seat, the men on the ground were working hard to remove all of the fake trees that they'd positioned over the runway, which had obscured it from being spotted by enemy reconnaissance. It wasn't long before the runway was cleared and the SS captain gave the pilot the orders to take off.

The engines of the plane roared to life, and the plane took off. Soon, it was off the ground and rose in the air as it started climbing up above the tree line. They didn't want to be seen by any enemy aircraft, so they remained low to the ground.

When Captain Otter was sure that the plane was safely on its way, he headed back towards the secret entrance to assist the general, who was waiting for his return, no doubt. There was a lot of work to be done, he thought to himself, as he climbed back into the fake stump.

Twenty minutes later, back on the German coastline and many miles away from the base, Lieutenant Colonel Plante and the rest of The 5th SAS Attack Force heard something that wasn't a bomber's engine flying towards them at just above tree level. The lead man on the patrol stopped and crouched down as he halted everyone.

Soon, Corporal Babcock spotted the plane as it flew only 250 feet above the ground. They could make out that it wasn't a German fighter and that it could hold several people onboard. This told them that somewhere between where they were now and the blown-up section of the mountainside was a secret landing strip.

"Somebody's trying to get away without being seen," Plante said to Sergeant Mitchell, who was kneeling not too far away from him. He nodded and returned to watching his arc of fire in case a German soldier suddenly popped up out of a hidden trench and started shooting at them. Everyone was focused and professional.

"Sir, no doubt, whoever is inside it has a very good reason for leaving without an escort. Probably to not get any attention from the allied bombers, I'd say," replied the commander.

Maybe the plane was carrying VIPs or important documents that the Germans didn't want to see the allies get if they got into the underground base. They'd only find out if that plane got shot down, thought Plante as he watched the plane continue onwards.

Somebody else had spotted the plane too. A British bomber that was losing altitude after being riddled with bullets from a very angry German fighter pilot spotted the plane as it headed towards the centre of Germany. One of the machine gunners on board the doomed bomber was Corporal Jonathan Kelly, who spotted the Nazi aircraft and took it upon himself to take it out before they crashed into either the sea or the forest below them.

He fired his weapon and shot his tracers towards it as he regained his balance for s few short seconds. Several moments went by with Kelly focusing on putting the tracer rounds onto his new target before his own plane crashed into the forest, creating a massive fireball and lighting up the area. The gunner no doubt had a smile on his face, though, before he had died as he saw the German plane go down somewhere near the German coastline.

The SAS patrol watched their arcs of fire while everyone there processed what they'd just witnessed. They scanned the sky for signs of parachutes, but no one had gotten out of the British bomber it seemed. Corporal Babcock hoped the gunner's dedication would yield results, but he didn't think they'd be the ones tracking the shot down German plane because it had landed in the wrong direction.

Lieutenant Colonel Plante was hoping that he would be able to salvage something from the Nazi plane wreckage too, but he would hand the task to the Royal Marine commandos as soon as they met up with the platoon that was supposed to meet them at their next objective, which was only five to six hundred yards north.

They needed to haul ass and hook up with them, he thought as he ordered the patrol to resume moving forwards. As he gave the order to move out, Babcock took the lead position of the patrol, which kept their spacing and watched their foot placements as they moved through the dense forest, as it had a lot of broken limbs on the ground from the storm that had raged so ferociously only a few hours ago.

Chapter 4

"Did you see those balls of light in the sky?" Lieutenant Colonel Plante asked Major Wilcock, the Royal Marine's platoon commander, as they met to discuss the next objective.

"I saw them, sir. Shit, we *all* saw them, but damn if I know what they were. It's some kind of Nazi super weapon that we don't have. That should be reported sir, even if we don't understand what it was," replied the major.

The SAS commander looked into Major Wilcock's eyes and nodded. "I'll do that. Don't you worry. We weren't expecting that plane to be shot down, though, and they didn't have an escort, which means they were trying to get away unnoticed. There could be something in that wreckage for us to find, so I want you to send some of your men to find it—somewhere towards the coastline—and see what they can recover. I want them to head out there now, and we'll move forward to our objective. They can re-join us later if we give them a new rendezvous point where they can find us, and then they can guard our escape route out of the underground base. Questions, Major?"

The major looked at his map and realized that the patrol he would dispatch on the new mission would need time to go back towards the coast and even more time to find and re-join their main fighting force later on. He looked up at his superior officer and said, "We'll have to make sure we have people at the ORV waiting for them, sir."

Lieutenant Colonel Plante looked at the major as he nodded in agreement. "Okay. No argument from me. Establish a spot where they know where to find us. The day is here, and we need to move on towards our objective major. Make sure you send some snipers out with that group so they can cover their patrol. I expect that there's going to be a beehive of activity in these forests soon—and for us as well as soon as we get to the impact zone."

Wilcock folded his map after writing down an eight-figure grid reference for the soldiers he would be sending out on the recovery mission. "Well, sir, we know that a plane took off from a landing strip not too far away from the mountain that was bombed, so there has to be an entrance near there somewhere. We need to find that airstrip, but it's going to be a hell of a patrol to reach it, he commented."

Plante stood up and picked up his weapon. "We'll find it. Go and brief your men that you want to send out on the new mission. I want the main group to leave here in thirty minutes and you can send your team that you pick for the recovery mission on its way before then if you'd like to. I'm going to brief my guys, and I'll let you know when we're heading off. Any further questions, Major?"

The major folded up his map and said, "None sir. I'll get everyone ready."

"Very good," replied the SAS officer. Plante then picked up his webbing and walked back to his group. The men were all in position, covering their arcs of fire while the O-group had been taking place. When he reached them, he called everyone over and began his briefing about the new plans and the route he'd decided to take in order to reach the underground base.

When he finished his warning order, everyone knew that they were heading towards the hidden airstrip and that they were to expect Nazis to be dug in and prepared for a fight, so he hoped that they would be able to observe the target area for a while before attacking anything. There were eight SAS members on the patrol—more than enough manpower to observe the ground—but on this mission, they would also go underground, which meant that they needed backup. There were sixteen Royal Marines that could still join them on the mission, taking the grand total to twenty-four with the other group of eight commandos, who would hopefully be back to meet up with them and become their reserve.

Plante was happy with these numbers. To accomplish the mission to infiltrate the underground base, they needed to find an entrance, and that would be like finding a needle in a haystack. With so much forest debris scattered about after the bombing, moving around stealthily could prove very difficult.

All it would take to alert a German sentry would be the snap of a twig, and when the Germans realized that the allies were approaching, the element of surprise would be gone. Therefore, Plante made sure that his men knew what was at stake and ordered them to be on high alert.

Plante saw the eight Royal Marines set off towards the coastline and knew that Major Wilcock would be ready to move with his remaining commandos, so he told his soldiers to get their Bergen's back on and to head out on the bearing he had given them. They would take the lead, and he would follow behind them with the Royal Marines.

There was a sense of urgency because, sooner or later, German ground troops would be all over the area. It was only a matter of time before hunter teams got sent out to search for survivors of the air battle that had raged through the previous night.

Several hours went by, and they were now moving through some dense forest, but things were expected to become way more difficult because they had to ascend a mountain. As Corporal Babcock tried to look for an alternate route, a deer suddenly jumped out from behind several bushes that were off to his right.

Sergeant Mitchell, who was behind him, raised his weapon. Then, he breathed in for three seconds and held it for another three. He exhaled and then repeated the process as he reacted to the dynamic stress that had been caused. He recognized that the deer was of no threat and raised his hand to stop their patrol so that the deer could move along without disturbing the birds in the local area. The last thing he wanted to see happen was a bunch of blackbirds squawking and alerting the Germans that some kind of predator was moving through the woods.

Meanwhile, the Royal Marines who had been sent out towards the coastline were having an equally hard go at it as they made their way through unfamiliar surroundings. When Corporal Brown, the lead man of the patrol group, spotted the smoke hovering in the air in between the tree branches in front of him, he put his hand up and closed a fist, which signalled to the rest of the patrol that they needed to stop and cover their arcs of fire as they studied the countryside for enemy movement.

A few moments of silence went by, and soon they all smelled the smoke and knew it was from something manmade. Sergeant O'Connor, who was in charge of the group, moved up to the point man and signalled for him to move forwards and see what was in the clearing up ahead. Carefully, Corporal Brown moved through the bush, hiding his advance behind the big trees. He took ten minutes to get up a bit of a hill, and then he was better able to see what was out in the clearing.

Sergeant Brown looked at his watch and saw that it was 6 p.m. It was going to get dark soon, and they needed to clear the site and take whatever they could find of value before dark. He didn't know what they would find as he watched his point man start to move towards the edge of the forest. He shifted his gaze behind him and signalled for his sniper to move up and find a position where he could provide covering fire as the rest of the group started to head to where Brown was situated.

Private Tilley, the sniper, gave O'Connor a thumbs up and moved off in the direction that he had been instructed to head towards via hand signals. Sergeant O'Connor continued to point in the direction Tilley was to move towards as he watched the other soldiers move past him. They were being silent and professional. No one was making a noise as Tilley continued on his way to find a place where he would be able to take out any enemy forces without being seen.

By 1800 hours, O'Connor had his group at the edge of the forest, overlooking the meadow. They could see that the Nazi plane had crashed and that there was a considerable debris field behind it, but the body of the craft was still in one piece and there was smoke still coming out of it. Corporal Brown approached the wreckage, being careful to watch out for survivors.

The burnt metal, wires, and fuel gave off a distinct artificial smell that drew them in. As more of the Royal Marines left the cover of the forest, they checked their arcs of fire and watched for enemy movement in all directions. Meanwhile, Tilley was set up beside a tree, watching the others search for anything salvageable at the crash site through his riflescope.

Back out on the open sea, Captain Kurt Sommer was looking at several lights that he could see off in the distance from the wheelhouse of his medium-sized fishing trawler, which measured forty-eight feet from end to end. He pointed at the lights, wondering what they were. "Do you see that?" the captain asked his first mate as he pointed out into the darkness in front of the main window of the wheelhouse. Derek Lang looked at the map on the wall and out the main window too. He saw the German Navy ship's light and then its silhouette off in the distance. "That's not a star. That's a bright light from a ship. Germans!"

Quickly, the captain took hold of the steering wheel and turned the boat so that only one side of his vessel could be seen. The first mate walked towards the door rather quickly, but as he did, he smelled the vomit bucket that still hadn't been emptied, and it was a third full. "I can dump that bucket over the rails on the way," he offered, but Captain Sommer shook his head. "There's not enough time. Focus on the things you need to be focused on," he replied.

Derek knew the drill, but now he also had to worry about getting the rescued airmen suited up and in the water before they were boarded. He turned towards his captain and said, "Wish me luck. How much time do you think we have before they reach us?"

Sommer looked back out the main window and thought for a second. "They're headed for us right now, so they know we're out here. I'd say you have maybe ten minutes—maybe fifteen at most. Make sure everything's hidden while they're getting suited up. I'm moving the boat so they only see one side of us," replied the captain.

It didn't take long for the first mate to reach the door that went down into the galley and the crew's quarters where they'd put the two men they'd fished out from the sea after they had watched the bomber crash into the ocean after being swarmed by the glowing balls of light the night before. They still hadn't talked about that, but he was looking forward to seeing if the survivors had any ideas as to what they had been. But for now, Kurt needed to figure out if the radio was safely hidden away and wouldn't be discovered by the crew members that were about to board their vessel.

He opened the door and climbed down the stairs. He saw the two British airmen in the galley drinking coffee. They saw him and wondered what was on his mind as he walked over to a closet and pulled out two rubber diver's suits. "Germans approaching. We can't hide you on the boat. Take some butter from the icebox and cover yourselves with it. Then, put these on. You're going over the side, and you only have five minutes to put them on. Keep your wool socks on, and drink up that coffee so you stay warm. These suits were given to us by the British. They're experimental suits," he said.

Sergeant Parker looked at the first mate with disbelief in his eyes. "You've got to be bloody joking, he said as he watched Kurt Lang disappear into another room. Before he disappeared completely, he looked back at them and said, "I have to make sure certain things are hidden, and I don't have time to talk. Put your shoes on the table. I have to throw them overboard along with your uniforms. You have four minutes. They'll be here in seven, and by then, you need to be in the water!" Corporal Thompson looked shocked. "That water's bloody freezing, mate. We won't survive in there for very long," he stated defiantly. All he heard were noises in the other room. Quickly, they shared the butter, covering themselves in it, and then they got into the suits without any further complaint.

When Lang came back out, the two recovered airmen were looking like a pair of seals. He saw their uniforms and grabbed them. "Okay, there's a hose underneath the boat in the middle of the ship. You must swim underneath the boat and find it. We've created a chamber where you can share the breathing tube between you, and there are also some metal loops welded to the hull that you can hold onto should we have to move the boat. The tube runs through the boat and up the flagpole, so they won't see it. You've gotta' hold on to those metal loops no matter what, fellas. Wait until you hear me banging on the bottom of the engine room six times in a row, and then you can come up. The Germans will be boarding us and searching every corner of this ship so it's important that you don't come up to the surface until you hear my signal. You'll be totally submerged in darkness and the water will be bloody cold. That's why you put the butter over your skin. It'll help as a barrier," explained the first mate.

Sergeant Parker was quite nervous and asked the next question while putting his shoes on the table as he'd been directed to do. "How long do you think we'll be down there?"

Derek shrugged his shoulders. "I'd hate to guess, but you'll be under there until they leave. Could be fifteen minutes. Could be an hour. I can't honestly tell you. Keep watching one another for signs of severe hypothermia, and do whatever you can to keep yourselves from passing out from the cold. Remember, the air tube is in the middle of the boat, and it's dangling out there right now. You have to suck in the air and then blow it out—then share the tube with the other person. Now, if there are no further questions, you have only minutes until they get here. Let's go," Kurt said as he tied a brick attached to a rope which he began wrapping around their military clothing and their shoes.

When they got outside, they could hear someone speaking loudly over some kind of loudspeaker, which was coming from the opposite side of the boat. They had a spotlight on Captain Sommer's boat, but they couldn't see Lang or the two airmen as they crept over to the rails and climbed down into the frigid waters. Kurt quickly let the clothing sink as the two airmen slipped into the water. "Jesus! This is fucking freezing!" Corporal Thompson said.

Lang raised one of his fingers to his mouth. "Shhhh! Go under the boat. The engine's stopped, so the Germans can board us. Go there now. Remember not to come up until after you hear me make three loud bangs on the hull. Go! Hurry!"

With the orders given, the two airmen submerged themselves beneath the waves of the dark turbulent ocean and disappeared.

It wasn't a moment too soon, as the German Navy Frigate came along side and drove around the boat that very moment. They saw Lang walking towards the wheelhouse. Even though the weather wasn't working in their favour, the Navy vessel had no problems being out there.

As Captain Sommer watched from the wheelhouse, several sailors in the German vessel lowered a skiff and got into it. Then, they came over to the *Blue Gem*, and Lang secured the lines to their boat as they climbed aboard.

A few minutes later, a young lieutenant walked up to the wheelhouse after Lang pointed towards the captain. A petty officer stayed with him and issued orders to several of his crew to go below deck and look around to see if they could find any contraband while the petty officer started asking the first mate a variety of questions. For ten minutes, the petty officer interrogated Derek as the rain-soaked into his clothing, making him shiver. Finally, the petty officer accepted his answers and allowed himself to be escorted below deck so he could inspect all the rooms himself.

In the wheelhouse, the young lieutenant asked Captain Sommer similar questions. Why was he was out at sea so late at night? Did he have a permit to fish in these waters? Why only two crew members? Sommer remained calm and did his best to answer the young officer's questions. The officer inspected his paperwork and saw that he had the correct permits to be out on the sea fishing for his quota. He was satisfied that they were in order, and he handed it all back to Kurt.

Sommer took the paperwork and put it in a small desk drawer that was in a corner of the wheelhouse while the lieutenant looked out the main window to see what his crew was doing outside on the main deck. "It doesn't seem like there's anything out of the ordinary going on here. Have you seen anything that you feel you should be report to us since you have been out here for so long, Captain?"

The navy lieutenant studied Sommer's face for signs that he might be lying about something after he asked the question. Kurt turned towards him and shook his head. "No, Lieutenant. The seas have been so rough that my total focus has been to prevent water from getting into the engine room. We did a basic repair on an old engine, as I didn't expect the storm to last this long or be so treacherous. As soon as we catch our quota, we'll be returning to port," he answered.

Satisfied with his answers, the officer looked around and saw the vomit bucket in the corner with the wet towels in it. He pointed to it and said, "I can smell that. It must be full. I can't imagine what it must have been like for you in that storm that we just had. We had trouble on our boat too, but ours was much bigger than yours. The stench in this wheelhouse is going to have an effect on your judgment. You should give this place a cleaning as soon as you can. I am satisfied with your paperwork. Your orders are to catch your quota and then return to port. Do you have any other questions for me, Captain?"

The captain of the *Blue Gem* shook his head, and the lieutenant then walked out of the wheelhouse. He stepped onto the main deck, where he called out for his men to get back to the boat that they'd come over in. His men heard him and complied with his orders straightaway.

As they got into their boat, Derek Lang, the first mate of the fishing boat, untied the lines and held their bowline firmly until everyone was onboard the small skiff. Then, he tossed the rope at one of the crew members in the boat and waved them off as they returned to their vessel. As Captain Sommer watched from the wheelhouse, the rain continued to come down, but he was still able to see his first mate that was now walking back towards the wheelhouse. A few moments later, he was inside and talking to his captain again. "They didn't find the radio?" Sommer asked curiously.

Lang shook his head. "No. How long have they been underwater?"

Captain Sommer looked at his watch. It was 8 p.m. "They've been under the boat for twenty-seven minutes. They must be dead by now," he replied in all seriousness. "We have to untie their ship and leave the area before we can get them out from underneath the boat. Go down to the galley, and get a pot of coffee on the boil. They have their wetsuits on, so they should be able to survive for a little longer, though they'll be icicles by now," Sommer replied.

The first mate agreed and noticed how much it stunk in the wheelhouse. "Give me the sick bucket. I'll dump it over the side. I think it's safe enough for me to do that now. I bet the lieutenant wasn't too impressed with that," Lang commented.

Kurt laughed. "No. He wasn't impressed by it at all, but it made him want to leave the ship as quickly as possible, so it helped us quite a bit I'd say. Take it and dump it over the side, Derek. After you get the coffee made, come back and check with me. If I say it's all clear, we'll get them out of the water and get some coffee into them straightaway," he said.

"They're lucky we saw their plane crash. If we hadn't seen the parachutes, they'd be shark bait," Derek said jokingly.

"Don't kid yourself. We may only pull up an arm and a leg since they've been under the water for so long. I hope they're okay, though. We'll soon see," replied captain Sommer as Lang took hold of the sick bucket and left the wheelhouse.

By the time the captain and the first mate got the two airmen out of the water, they were severely hypothermic and couldn't even stand on their own. They were close to unconsciousness, and it took a monumental effort to haul them back up onto the deck from the sea. The hidden compartment with the hose that housed their air supply had saved their lives, but they would talk about that later when the almost unconscious men could talk intelligibly again.

The only way they could haul them in was to get the two men to hold onto a fishing net that Lang put over the side for them. Luckily for everyone, the navy patrol boat didn't return, and they were able to get the airmen onto the main deck and drag them below, one man at a time.

After the second man was brought downstairs, their wetsuits came off and the men held onto hot wet rags for a good minute before placing them in their armpits and then onto their faces to warm up just a touch. They didn't look good when the captain stared at them closely. They were barely shivering, which meant their bodies were shutting down. "Go and get them some of that coffee, but cool it down a little. Let's warm them up from the inside out," he said.

It was going to be touch and go for the next while, but it was too dangerous to get the radio out. They needed to focus on bringing these men back to consciousness, and after that happened, they could start making plans.

Chapter 5

Deep in the underground base, the German intelligence officer left to find the second-highest-ranking officer to inform him of some grizzly news. General Matz had been killed due to a collapsed tunnel, and now he had just learned that the SS captain that had flown out of there the night before hadn't made it to his destination and was presumed to have been shot down somewhere en route to Himmler's castle. Captain Otter had to venture down to the lower levels, where the real secrets were situated, to brief the new base commander.

Before he went down the stairs that would take him to the lowest level, he saw prisoners working to clean up the debris littered on the floors of the uppermost tunnels as guards barked orders at them. The Allies had had some success in damaging the infrastructure.

Several engineers were studying the cracks in the walls caused by bombs as Otter looked to see what they were up to before going down the stairs. There was a strong chance that their ammunition stockpiles were at risk, but he would inspect those rooms after he had dealt with informing the new base commander that General Matz had been killed only an hour ago.

At the bottom of the long stairway were two German guards that were waiting for anyone coming down the stairway. The intelligence officer showed his ID and was allowed to go into the highly secure area. As he walked down the well-lit tunnel, he looked for signs of cracks in the walls but didn't see any damage. In front of him were several offices, storage rooms, and another staircase that took people down to a large open cavern where a large channel of water and a dock were situated.

As he looked out over the underground facility, he could see the multitude of Navy personnel working hard to move the secret items that had been put in dozens of crates and metal drums. It almost looked like an ant colony.

Otter stopped once he reached the office of Rear-Admiral Heinz. He opened the door and went inside and was immediately met with the gaze of the liaison officer who was working diligently behind a desk. "Captain Otter. Do you have news for the rear admiral? He isn't here right now," he said.

The intelligence officer closed the door and walked up to the desk of Captain Schmidt. "Where is he? I have to tell him important things that are quite urgent, I'm afraid." The liaison officer offered Otter a chair, and the intelligence officer sat down to discuss the matter further. He looked Schmidt in the eyes and let out a deep breath. "General Matz was killed a short while ago. The bombs managed to penetrate down to our floor, and debris fell from the ceiling. A section of tunnel collapsed and killed fifteen people in the headquarters section. I wasn't around him at the time, which is why I'm still alive," he explained.Schmidt looked shocked. "We've had reports of some trembling from the bombing down at your level, but I had no idea that the allies had bombs that would reach down so far. We're beneath hundreds of feet of granite. We're hundreds of feet from the surface. How is that even possible?"

Captain Otter shook his head. "They've obviously been working on their bombs. They produced shock waves that managed to get all the way down to our level. I'm glad that they didn't reach yours, though. I've come to inform the rear admiral that he is now the ranking officer for the entire base, and I was hoping to get some orders from him right away. Can you locate him, please? I realize that the army is in charge of the security operations above your level, but I need to have a conversation with Heinz first," he stated firmly.

The liaison officer stood up and put his hat on his head. "Under these circumstances, I don't think that he would object if we were to go and find him. I know where he was going. Follow me," he said as he walked away from his desk. Both of the men then left the office and went down the staircase that led to the open area below them.

It took them another fifteen minutes of checking places before they found the rear admiral. He was busy inspecting the mercury. He wanted to make sure that they were sealed and wouldn't leak on their next voyage out to sea. The rear admiral was asking the commodore who was in charge of this task a lot of questions, so they patiently waited off to the side until the right moment came.

After the commodore answered his questions, the rear admiral gave the go-ahead to start storing the sealed metal drums in a secure storage room not far away and ordered that a guard be positioned there to monitor their safety. With the new orders given to him, the commodore saluted his senior officer, and the rear admiral returned the salute. He then started walking away from him, and as he did, he locked eyes with his liaison officer who was standing beside Captain Otter.

The rear admiral waited until he was closer to them, and then he wanted to know what had brought Captain Otter down to the lower levels. He wasn't mincing words, well-known for getting straight to the point.

"Sir, I've come to inform you that there has been an accident and that General Matz has been killed," replied Captain Otter. The news stopped the rear admiral in his tracks. "What? How?"

The intelligence officer looked down at the cement floor and then shook his head with disappointment. "The Allies have developed bombs that can penetrate underground to very deep levels. They cracked the walls on our first two levels, and a section of tunnel collapsed. The people that were under the area in question did not survive. So, I have been trying to figure out who is the highest-ranking officer in our underground base, sir, and that person is you. I am prepared to suggest that you must take over command and provide me with orders. I also have an intelligence briefing to give you. Can we go back to your office, please?"

The rear admiral nodded but didn't say anything. He was stunned by the news. General Matz was a good officer, and he would be missed, Heinz thought as they started walking towards the stairs that led back up to the offices. Otter didn't spend a lot of time down where they were because this was strictly a navy operation. He was amazed at how efficient everything seemed. People were busy working on a variety of jobs. There were many people putting things into crates while others were getting ready to seal them up.

"Your men work very hard down here, sir. Everyone seems to know their job and what's expected of them," Otter said as they got closer to the stairs. The rear admiral looked behind him to make sure that Otter was right. When he was satisfied by what he saw, he nodded his head and then said, "Yes. Well, we're on a strict timeline. We have to get everything we have down here shipped off on the next U-boat that's able to get in here, and who knows when that will be with everything going on above us as it is right now. Is there much damage on the surface? Has anyone been sent to take a look at what they've done? I want to know how they found out about us. We're so deep in the mountains. Nobody was supposed to find out about our secret facilities down here. Perhaps a double agent is working in our midst? A mole perhaps or maybe one of the prisoners has escaped? I want head counts done as soon as possible," he concluded.

Captain Otter reached the entranceway to the stairs and walked by one of the guards who had been positioned there. He was armed and ready to challenge anyone coming or going, and under the circumstances, it seemed like a good thing to do. Otter waited until they were out of the staircase before he answered the colonel's many questions.

"We don't have that information, sir, but these are all sensitive questions that require further investigation. We must look at every single person working here. As for the surface, there's a group guarding the landing strip, but I'm unsure if we actually did send anyone out there to hunt for British crews that were shot down. I know that our secret weapons did cause significant casualties though. That's come from the senior officer in charge of security at the landing strip. He has reported that at least a dozen allied bombers were destroyed as they attacked us," Captain Otter explained as they continued to walk towards the rear admiral's office.

Shortly after midnight on the twenty-ninth of March, the fake stump near the secret German landing strip opened up again. This time, dozens of soldiers started to climb out of it one at a time. A sentry on duty soon saw a group starting to form and notified Major Wagner, the senior officer who was in charge of the security forces that were protecting the covert landing strip. He walked over to the soldiers coming out from the artificial stump and identified himself. He pointed to where they could hide until all of them were safely out of the tunnel system, and then he stayed near the stump, carefully briefing each soldier that exited the tunnel system where they needed to go next.

It took just over an hour for sixty men to exit and come up to the surface. The major then briefed the men and the junior officers on what their mission would be. They were to act as a hunter force—to go out and ascertain the damage and to try and find any surviving British aircrews that were attempting to escape Germany. Wagner was startled, however, when three dogs came out as they were lifted one by one very carefully with the help of small pieces of cargo netting. If there were any survivors out there, surely these soldiers would track them down, he thought as he watched the junior officers take command of their soldiers and move out into the forest under the cover of darkness. The major made sure that they went in different directions. Some were heading towards the border with Belgium while others were headed back towards the ocean and the coastline along the border with the Netherlands.

At 8 a.m. that same day, Vera Atkins walked down Baker Street in London's business district and entered a building that didn't look out of the ordinary. However, once she went through the main doors, she was under the watchful eye of several men who wanted to see her identification and search through her purse, which she voluntarily presented to them.

She looked around and saw that there was a lot of hustle and bustle going on, and that was to be expected. There were a lot of things going on at the moment for the special operations executive, and she was about to get a briefing, herself, at 8:30 on the main floor of their headquarters.

"You're all clear, Ms Atkins. Thank you. Here's your purse," the head of security said to her. She accepted her purse with a smile and said, "Thank you," then continued onwards down the hall. Her office was upstairs on the second floor of the building, and so she went to the stairs and started working her way up.

A few minutes later, she was on her way down to her office and saw that her secretary was already there, making them both a hot cup of tea before she had to go off to fetch her boss—Maurice Buckmaster. "Good morning, Margaret. How are you this morning?" she asked.

Her secretary turned around and looked at Vera, smiling cordially. "Oh, good morning. I'm doing well, thank you. Tea's nearly ready and I have several messages for you, but don't forget about your early morning meeting downstairs."

Vera walked over to her secretary's desk and looked at the messages while Margaret poured them both a cup of tea. She would return those calls later when she had a moment to spare. "Have you seen Maurice come in this morning, or do I need to phone his wife to make sure he's on his way?"

Margaret followed her boss as she walked into the office. While Vera put her coat on the coat rack Margaret Palmer put Vera's cup of tea on her desk for her. "I haven't seen Mr Buckmaster come in yet would you like me to ring his house?"

Vera smiled back at her secretary as she walked over to her own desk and took a sip of her tea. "Yes please, dear. He can't be late for that meeting. He asked me to remind him, and that's what I need you to do if he's not here in five more minutes. I don't want to jump the gun just yet, so we'll give him a little more time to show up."

Margaret smiled as she walked out of her office. "Not a problem. I'll walk over to his office and see if he's there for you." Vera put down her cup of tea and sat down behind her desk. The weather outside her window looked pretty bleak. She saw Margaret was almost out the door when she realized she hadn't thanked her for making the tea. "Oh, sorry, Margaret. I have a lot going on in my mind. Thanks for making the tea and for checking if he's there for me."

Margaret began shutting Vera's door and replied, "You're quite welcome. I'll let you know if he's there or not. I'm away from my desk, so please pick up the phone if it rings."

Vera nodded her head in agreement. "Most certainly. Thank you," she said, then looked back down at her desk. The door closed, and Vera took a key out from her pocket and unlocked the drawer, which held a manila folder inside. She took it out and began reviewing the contents as she sipped her tea. She tried to distract herself while waiting on the news of where Maurice was at the present moment.

There were pictures of several women that she looked at as well as profiles for each of them. She had to start choosing whom she would allow to be trained as the next agents that would be dropped into France to be their eyes and ears. She kept herself busy until her secretary returned and told her that Mr Buckmaster had finally shown up and was in his office. Relieved, she left her office and walked over to his after locking the manila folder back up in her desk drawer.

By 8:25, Vera and Maurice entered the briefing room downstairs. Maurice walked in and was quickly noticed by S.O.E. Agent James Walker, who was standing in front of a podium. "Good morning Maurice. Morning Vera," he said with a gracious smile.

The two members from F-Section then sat down and waited for the meeting to start. There were only a few others in the room, but Vera wasn't expecting there to be a lot of people since this was all about the operation in Germany and it had been highly classified.

James got the meeting going at half past the hour. He closed the door after one other person showed up, who apologized for running late and quickly sat down at the back of the room. "I'm ready to start," said James, walking back to the podium. "Thank you for coming."

When James was in front of the 8 people in the room he smiled at everyone and then started his briefing. "Okay, let's begin, shall we? We're all here to learn about the mission that was orchestrated on March 26 with an aerial bombing on what S.O.E. believes is an underground base that's located in Germany but is very close to the borders of the Netherlands and Belgium. From the reports that we've received from returning pilots, it seems that a number of things happened. The good news is that the bombs fell on target and there was very little resistance initially. The bad news is that when the Germans did fight back, they may have used some kind of high-tech weapon that we've never seen before. The aircrews have called what they observed a 'foo fighter.' Apparently, there were dozens of light balls flying in unheard-of patterns. That's the best description we have at this point. Were they manned? We don't have the answer to that question right now, but these things interfered with our planes and caused them to crash into each other. The reports are that we sent forty-eight bombers on the mission and only half of them made it back."

"What about the distractions you had planned?" Maurice asked.

James nodded and then answered the question. "We did have distractions. We set up false raids, and we had saboteurs blowing up train tracks in Germany. We had bridges being blown up in France. We had other bombers flying missions in Nazi-occupied Belgium. We had other bombing missions on other German coastal cities too. However, we were short on manpower because we had so many attacks going on at the same time. The submarines that we put out there were constantly looking for U-boat wolfpacks while at the same time relaying information and helping us drop off Royal Marine commandos who were supporting our newly created SAS Regiment in Belgium. The British submarines had standing orders to stick around the area in case they were needed to extract our Special Forces people. We had three working on this mission. Two we've heard from, but one has not reported back to us in some time, and there's the possibility that they've been taken out."

Another SOE agent wanted to ask a question, and James let him do so. "Sir, what about the underground base? Did you confirm that there's something there?"

James hesitated and collected his thoughts. "No. Nothing confirmed as of yet. We haven't heard anything back from the Special Forces we sent in. I know that will disappoint you, Maurice, but I haven't had any information come to me yet from Lieutenant Colonel Plante, who's in charge of the ground forces heading towards that underground base. My understanding is that they're mainly resistance members from Belgium, France, and other areas of the British military who have Belgian ancestry. As such, they're somewhat untested as a unit. I hope everything's going to go well for them. Time will tell. I expect that we'll hear from them soon, and based on the information we receive, we'll act accordingly. So, since we don't have closure yet on the success of the ground mission, we'll have to have a second briefing. I'll notify you in forty-eight hours or less about that. If you have questions, please realize I don't have a lot of information yet. But if you have any, let me try and answer them."

The meeting didn't last much longer after that. When Maurice and Vera left the briefing room for their offices on the second floor, they weren't pleased with the lack of information. They didn't talk much until they got up to the second floor, at which point Maurice walked down to his office and invited Vera to go through the door first. After she was inside, Maurice shut the door so they could have some privacy.

Maurice sat down in the chair behind his desk and then looked at Vera, who was sitting in a chair on the other side of the desk. "What do you think of all this, Vera?"

Ms Atkins shook her head and breathed out a heavy sigh. "Our resistance members are precious. We only have limited resources in France right now. Why did we let ourselves be a part of this mission?

Maurice thought about the question. It was a good point. Then, he leaned back in his chair and pondered before letting out a deep sigh. "British S.O.E. came to me and asked for manpower for this mission. They've provided us with a lot. It was our turn to help them, and I was then told that there was something underground there. I heard that they employed Aleister Crowley and used his remote viewing techniques. That's how they got Hess to fly to Scotland in 1941, so they wanted to find out if Crowley could see anything underground in Germany, and apparently, he was successful at it. The head of the British branch of SOE said that if they could get down inside that underground base, we would learn of things that we had no idea the Nazis were developing," he explained to Vera, who was sitting in the chair across from him with a wide-eyed expression on her face.

She was amazed by what her boss had just told her. "Are you saying that they employed a psychic to find out if there were underground factories in Germany? Are you out of your mind?"

Maurice chuckled and shook his head before he replied. "I'm no more out of my mind than Hitler, who believes in collecting ancient relics to give him the edge over us, Vera. You know as well as I do that he has people looking for artefacts all over the world right now. Just about every leader on the planet uses some sort of psychic or has their charts read or something to that effect. It's been happening since antiquity, and it's not about to stop, so yes, British Intelligence employed Aleister Crowley to find out about the underground factories using his methods. He came up with several targets, including a big one over in Poland but we haven't done anything about that one yet. We sent our forces into Germany and time will tell us what they've discovered," he explained in a confident tone.

Vera didn't know what to say. She remained silent for several seconds and looked around the room as she tried to think about something positive to say. Then, Maurice spoke again before she could reply.

"We have to stop them if they're that advanced, Vera. We all know that whatever the Germans make tends to last forever. They know how to build things efficiently. Imagine if we could take possession of what they have. That would be amazing. We could beat them at their own game."

Vera agreed with her boss. "Yes, well . . . I suppose it would be good if we confirmed that there was a secret underground base there. I just hope that we don't lose all of those soldiers that we worked so hard to put together. We need them back in France and Belgium. I have circuits of agents being dropped into small towns in France, and when it's time for them to leave, they need to have support to help them get out of the country."

Maurice heard her loud and clear. "How are your other agents doing? Are they reporting anything of significance?"

"I'm working on female agents right now as well as several supply drops to support their efforts and help the local resistance forces in their respective areas. I've had some reports indicating that they're moving people by train late at night. But I don't know where the Nazis are moving people to yet. I know that they're starting to build bases in certain rural areas, but I don't know if those will become death camps. Maybe they'll build underground facilities like they did in Germany?"

Maurice let out a sigh. "We're up against an evil force. Keep doing those missions, Vera. We'll have some more news soon. I'll call James and let him know what our concerns are."

Vera stood up and adjusted her sweater. "That's good. I'd appreciate you checking with James, and I'll keep those supply drop missions going, but I'm seeing us having a shortage of planes soon if we're not careful." She then walked out of the office and went back to hers.

At 2100 hours on March 29, Captain Otter climbed out of the fake stump near the hidden airstrip. As he looked around, he saw many German soldiers still working away to put fake trees back over their landing strip. It had managed to remain untouched by the British bombing mission, which meant it still hadn't been seen from the air. However, even days after the bombing raid by the British, the smell of the burnt forest was still quite strong.

Captain Otter found the major who was in charge of the landing strip and took in all the information that he wanted to tell him. He showed Captain Otter where the soldiers had been sent, and then Otter was taken to a place where he could better observe the damage that the bombs had done to the countryside. He couldn't see a great deal initially, but the lack of standing trees on the slope of the mountainside where the base was situated gave him a hell of an impression a few minutes later when he'd been taken to a better vantage point. The area was exposed and could easily be seen from the air if another bombing mission was to ever be sent back there. The landscape was peppered with large holes from all the bombs that had recently dropped.

"This is incredible. We're lucky that we only sustained moderate damage underground on the first few levels, Major. It could have been much worse. Lucky for us, we had the super weapons flying around to protect us. Hitler must be notified that they saved our base from what could have been catastrophic consequences."

The major looked at him and nodded. "What I want to know, Captain, is how they found out about this location. Very few people come and go. The soldiers here are on a permanent posting. Maybe we have a double agent?"

That gave the two men something to talk about, and for the next hour, they spoke discretely, away from other soldiers who were watching for enemy movement.

Unfortunately for them, the SAS were highly trained in observational skills and had already set up a location with two men observing the impact area as they watched for signs of German activity. Sergeant Mitchell had been demonstrating to Babcock how to stay still, explaining that eventually, the natural surroundings would accept them—and he was right, as several birds landed nearby to inspect the ground for their next meal, thinking that the humans were no more than strange-looking logs.

Babcock smiled as he spotted a deer come out from the trees to graze. He and Mitchell had been on observational duties for four hours, lying in the pronc position under some brush on the side of a mountain that overlooked the impact zone from the bombing run. The other six men from their patrol were behind them under the trees some thirty yards to their rear. Four men were sleeping while another two were on sentry. The Royal Marines were nowhere to be seen, though. That was because they'd gone out to meet up with their other section that had been sent to go and find the missing plane and its contents. They wouldn't be expected back for another forty-eight hours, so until then, they needed to keep a low profile and wait for their safe return.

"I think I see something," Babcock said as he looked through the binos. He focused on an area that was away from the impact zone because he had seen some flickering of light in his peripheral vision that didn't resemble flames. Someone had just lit a cigarette! As he watched, he could see someone smoking down in the valley beneath them. He couldn't believe the distance from which a cigarette could be seen at night. "Take a look, Sergeant. There's someone over there about a mile from the impact zone, smoking a fag. There's somebody on sentry. What are they protecting?"

Mitchell put down his canteen of instant coffee he'd just started to drink in order to warm himself up. He took the binoculars from Babcock and looked in the direction that Carl had pointed him towards. They were both quiet for about thirty seconds, and then the sergeant started looking around some more. "I think we might have found our entry point. They're protecting something, and I think I'm making out some kind of overhead protection. We need to get closer or stay here and observe that position during the day tomorrow. You're right about there being a sentry, but I think I see more than one soldier down there. They have people in that area who seem stationary. Maybe they're guarding an entrance into the tunnels? Go back and get the C.O. and tell him what we've found while I keep watching," Sergeant Mitchell ordered.

"Right. Not a problem, Sergeant. I'll go and get him and send him forwards. Do you want me to come back with him?" Babcock asked.

The sergeant shook his head. "Nah, mate. You're good. Go and get some sleep and ask Plante to come up and take over the rest of your shift," the sergeant stated as he continued to look through the binoculars.

Babcock then moved back slowly into the rear area. As he made his way back through the darkness, a cold wind blew through the trees. He watched as some of the old-growth rocked back and forth, creaking and making slight noises. The guys that were sleeping had positioned themselves under those trees, and if any of their big branches broke off and fell down, they'd have one hell of a headache, he thought as he crawled back to the sleeping area to wake up Lieutenant Colonel Plante to deliver the message he'd been given.

One of the two men that were sleeping in the darkness beneath the trees suddenly heard a branch snap, and he immediately reached to his side and grabbed his submachine gun, aiming it in the direction where he'd heard the noise. He could see it was Corporal Babcock because of the light on his face, so he lowered his weapon. He stated the password challenge, and Babcock quickly replied with the correct answer, which made Corporal Oliver ease his thumb from the safety of his weapon. "What are you doing back here? Is it my shift already?" Oliver asked as the Commanding Officer poked his head out of his sleeping bag. "What's going on Corporal Babcock?" asked Plante.

Carl moved closer to the SAS commander so he didn't have to talk too loud. "Sir, we've spotted several sentries about a mile off from where the bombs went off. They're guarding something, and Sergeant Mitchell wanted me to come and tell you. He's requesting that you come up to the forward area and do some observations with him, sir," Babcock replied.

"Okay. Let me get out of this thing, and I'll go. You may as well stay here. I'll stay up and see what's going on," the patrol commander said as he unzipped his sleeping bag and crawled out into the brisk air. As he stood up, he could still smell smoke. "That forest down there is still smouldering. I bet they're going to have troops out there tonight putting those fires out."

"They probably will, sir. I just saw a sentry smoking a fag, and we're so far away from them. You can see the broken trees on the ground still burning down there when the wind hits them; the embers that are still smouldering glow red, and you can still see a lot of them around the impact areas," Babcock replied as he went over to his Bergen and got out his sleeping bag and ground sheet.

A minute went by and Plante was ready. He had his coat on as he moved forward into the darkness. The air was still quite chilly even though spring was trying to announce itself. There was still a fair bit of snow on the ground at this elevation, and the other sentries that were out guarding their positions still had their winter white camouflage on, which made them almost impossible to see, though they weren't very far away from where Oliver and Babcock were situated.

It didn't take the SAS commander very long to crawl up beside Sergeant Mitchell who was dead still as he watched what was going in the valley that was next to the side of the mountain that he had been bombed by the British on March 26.

"What's the story, Sergeant?

Mitchell handed his commander the binoculars and pointed in the direction he wanted him to look. "Over there, sir. If you stare at that area long enough you'll start to see that they have nets above their vehicles or whatever else they don't want us to see from the air. I'm betting on an entrance into the underground base because as far as I can tell, they think it's important enough to have several soldiers on sentry duty all around that position. Did Babcock tell you about the trees in the blast area still burning?"

Plante took the bino's from the sergeant and lay in the prone position beside him before he replied. "Yes, he did. He thought that the Germans would be sending troops to put them out so our bombers wouldn't see them if they came back," he said as he started looking around. It didn't take him very long to see what his sergeant was talking about. "I see a sentry. No. Make that two. I see two soldiers walking around. There's bound to be more of them."

Sergeant Mitchell adjusted his wool toque because it was getting itchy. "I think we need to get down closer and see what they're hiding, sir. Either that or we call in for a diversion so we can get down there and slip into the underground complex. Would it be such a bad idea if we requested that SOE go ahead with their second bombing mission to distract them?"

There was silence for a few more seconds before the senior officer replied. "We have another forty-eight hours before the major and his men are due back in the area to meet us. And we know that they sent a shitload of soldiers out into the woods to find the bombers that they managed to shoot down. I'd say they think everyone's on the run out of this area, so they're getting lazy. Might be a good time for us to send a team down there to see what we can find out. After we get the intel from that, then we can go ahead with their second bombing mission. It's not even late at night yet. If we avoid the snow, we could sneak down and watch them for a while. Pick up some conversations maybe? It's cold out. Those sentries are going to hang out and talk. Maybe they'll do what you say and go out into the impact areas to put out the burning embers. What time is it now?"

Mitchell looked at his watch. "It's just about twenty-one hundred hours sir."

Plante handed the binos back to Mitchell and said, "Okay, how about you take three men with you and sneak down there to set up a listening post? Be back here before sunrise, though. I don't want you to engage with them in any way. Just observe what they're doing. Find out what they're hiding, and look for that entrance. If we find it, then we're golden!"

"No problem, sir. I'll go back to the sleeping beauties and get them ready."

"Very good, sergeant. I'll stay here. Put one man on sentry, and have two others get some sleep. Tell them I'll stay here for another two hours and watch you descend into the red zone. Assign somebody to come and relieve me at twenty-three hundred hours. Good luck!" the Lieutenant Colonel replied as he watched Sergeant Mitchell nod back at him and then crawl back into the bush behind the forward position and return to where the others were situated.

On March 31, at 1300 hours, in another part of the forest—closer to the German coastline along the border with the Netherlands—Major Wilcock, the platoon commander for the Royal Marine Commandos was speaking with Sergeant Abbot to determine how much further they had to go before they reached their rendezvous point. "It's not very far, sir. Maybe an hour or two at most," Abbot replied as he pointed to the spot on the map. Suddenly, out of nowhere, rifle fire was heard. It was loud, and numerous machine guns and bolt-action riffles were being fired, indicating some kind of contact with the enemy.

Wilcock looked at Sergeant Abbott, and they both stood up without saying a word, each of them reacting instinctively. Returning to their sections, they ordered the men to head in the direction of the shooting, which seemed to still be a ways away from where they presently were.

The men quickly moved into an arrowhead formation and advanced cautiously through the woods. It was hard going because of the uneven ground, and several of the men tripped over deadfall, consequently making some unwelcome noises. This got a reaction from their platoon sergeant. "Careful, you bloody idiots! Be quiet!" Abbott then looked around at the men that he could see and gave hand signals to get the soldiers he was responsible for to put more distance between themselves. The forest was filled with loud explosions—a terrible cacophony. Grenades were being tossed somewhere off in the distance, and a firefight had commenced.

At the rear of their patrol, the major watched the woods for movement and saw several crows fly out of their hiding spot in the trees. They were frightened because of the machine guns, which were German. Towards the front of the arrowhead formation, Sergeant Abbot looked at the lead man and gave him more hand signals to continue forwards cautiously. The two sections of commandos tried their best not to make any further noise. But the major feared that the section he'd sent out to search for the crashed German plane a few days before had just been ambushed by the Germans.

Ten minutes later, the exchange of weaponry had reduced considerably. Abbot could tell that the Germans had gotten the upper hand and perhaps there were only one or two of the Royal Marines still alive in the engagement. There were still sub-machine guns firing though and that meant that the Germans were trying to pin down whoever was still alive that they had attacked or ambushed.

Major Wilcock gave his soldiers a hand signal to stop and cover their arcs of fire. Some were aiming their weapons up hills while others were hiding behind fallen trees and had arcs of fire that were straight in trajectory towards the front and the rear. "Take some water," he ordered as he gave a hand signal for the 2i/c to come over to him right away. As soon as Abbott saw the signal, he moved over to the major and had a talk with him.

"I think they've ambushed our guys," said Wilcock. I want to set up an ambush, ourselves, and kill as many of those bastards as we can. Maybe we'll get lucky and rescue a few of our men in the process. That rifle fire can't be more than half a mile in our forward direction. What do you think, Sergeant?" the major asked as he looked into Abbott's eyes.

"I think you're right, sir. If we set up a hasty ambush, I'd suggest we cover that higher ground, putting our snipers on each of the hills. Let them come towards us and when we see the whites of their eyes we'll take them out as they pass us. We'll hide behind the trees. I think they'll come this way shortly," Abbott replied.

"They'll have one or two of our men as prisoners. We need to make sure we don't shoot them. Make sure your men know. You take your section over there and get in a position where you and I can maintain hand signals with each other. You can be the lead section, and we'll hang back over there across the way, and we'll get them in a crossfire. But remember where we are and make damn sure your men know where we are too so they don't shoot at us. I'll let my guys know where you are. You give me the hand signal when you see them coming. We'll let them through. You let my section take out the front, and you take out the rear. It sounded like at least a platoon worth of soldiers. Maybe there's half that now, but they still have plenty of firepower. Tell the snipers to pick off the ones that try to escape. We can't allow them to get word back to their base that we're here. Any questions?"

Abbot shook his head. "No, sir."

Major Wilcock then gave him a nod and stood back up. He began walking over to his section and started briefing them while Sergeant Abbott went back to his soldiers and told them that they were setting up a hasty ambush and that they needed to check their ammo and get ready to move.

Chapter 6

At fifteen-thirty hours on March 13, Corporal Babcock spotted movement along a mountain ridge. He was on sentry duty with Corporal Oliver. As he looked through his binoculars, he saw German soldiers heading towards them and became alarmed. "I've got enemy movement!"

Oliver looked over at Carl and then looked in the direction that he was pointing at. He took his own binoculars out and then looked in the same direction. It took him a few seconds to find what Babcock was looking at, but soon he saw the Germans too. "I see at least six Germans," he said. "We'd better sound the alarm. It looks like the major and his men aren't coming back," Corporal Oliver replied as he slowly crawled back into the bushes and made his way to the patrol commander while Babcock remained, observing the enemy.

When Oliver found him in the rest area, he was sitting upright, looking at a topographical map. "Sir, we have enemy movement coming in our direction from a ridgeline that's above where we are. Babcock's got a visual and requests that you make your way over to his position," Corporal Oliver stated.

Lieutenant Colonel Plante then reached up and grabbed his weapon and went off on his own. As he passed Oliver, he looked at him and replied, "Alright. Get ready. We might have to bug out of here. Fold up my map for me please, Corporal. We've waited long enough for Major Wilcock and his men."

Sergeant Mitchell overheard the conversation and got the others ready to move. The men checked their weapons and then got their kit ready. "Get yourself sorted, Oliver!" The 2i/c ordered. "We're ready to move out of here in five minutes." Oliver nodded his head and went to his Bergen to make sure everything was in order.

A few minutes later, Corporal Babcock was showing his commanding officer where to look as he handed him the binos. "How many Germans did you see, Corporal?" his patrol commander asked, as he looked two-thirds up the mountain in front of them.

"I've counted at least six men, sir," Carl replied, watching Plante look through the binoculars as he lay in the prone position underneath the brush. Patiently the SAS commander observed the area while Babcock continued to observe the valley.

Suddenly, he was distracted by the movement of his commanding officer, who was now trying very hard to focus on what he was looking at.

"Corporal Babcock, I see your German soldiers, but I think I also see the major and quite a few of his men behind them. Take a look and tell me what you see. They're coming downhill so they can avoid what's down there. I think they've got prisoners," he said.

Babcock immediately shifted his gaze and started looking for the Royal Marines. A few seconds later, he had a visual. "Sir, I see a lot of soldiers. It's got to be Major Wilcock and his men. But why would they bring prisoners with them?" Babcock asked.

Plante stopped, looking up on the hillside behind their position. He turned around and went back into the brush and then into the forest where Sergeant Mitchell and the rest of the SAS patrol were eating a meal from their ration packs. "What would you say, Sergeant, if I told you that the major is up on that mountain behind me and he has prisoners with him?"

Mitchell shook his head. "I'd ask him why he brought prisoners when we're about to go down there. That makes no sense, sir," the 2i/c replied. The SAS commander nodded his head. "I agree with you. It doesn't make sense to me either, and I want you to go up to where I'm pointing right now and ask him directly. Take four men and leave the other two here. Bring the major back here. I want answers. Tell him what we found but do it away from those Germans so they don't hear what we know," he ordered.

"Right away, sir," Sergeant Mitchell replied as he picked the other three men who were to go with him as the SAS commander went back to join the forward OP.

The next morning as the sun came through the window of the Baker Street building, Vera Atkins walked over to the door of her boss who was in charge of F-Section and knocked after not finding his secretary at her desk. She usually escorted Vera into his office. "Enter," was the command that she heard, so she opened the door and walked in to see Maurice Buckmaster serving himself some tea. "Aw Vera, good of you to drop by," he said. "Can I offer you a fresh cup of tea?"

Vera let a large sigh and then said, "Have you forgotten about our meeting in fifteen minutes downstairs, sir? We have to get going soon or we'll be late for it, but I came here early so I could talk to you about something before we left your office," she explained.

He quickly looked over his shoulder and shook his head with disappointment. "Thank goodness for you, Vera. My memory isn't as good as it used to be," he said apologetically.

Vera knew this about him, though, which was why she'd gone to his office to fetch him in the first place. She showed him a file that she had underneath her arm.

Wondering what she had to say, he nodded. "Is that from one of your circuits in France?"

Vera nodded her head in response before replying. "The Nazis are so angry right now that they're searching high and low for our white mouse as they've dubbed her.".

Maurice offered a gentle smile, walking over to one of the chairs in the centre of his office and motioning for her to join him as he sat down with his cup of tea. "Why do they call her that I wonder," he asked as he placed his cup on the table in front of them.

Vera answered the question as she quickly sat herself down in a comfortable chair across from Maurice. "They call her the white mouse because she always manages to get away from them every time they put the squeeze on the area they suspect she might be hiding."

Maurice picked up his cup of tea and sipped from it as he watched Vera open up the file. She pointed to several of the typed reports within, then put them to one side, proceeding to place several pictures of women on the table between them.

As he looked at each picture, he saw that they were all in uniforms that belonged to the Women's Auxiliary Air Force. "Are these the women fully trained yet? I can see you've picked a whole group of ladies here. Why?"

Vera adjusted herself in the seat that was in front of Maurice and answered him. "They've all come from the W.A.A.F. because that's mostly where the women have been allowed to work to fight this war. We have over 150,000 women currently serving in many areas. I've gone through a lot of files, and these women have all been interviewed by myself and have met the requirements to be trained as operatives in France. They speak the language and are extremely intelligent. They can fly, and they have no children yet, so they can focus on the mission that they're assigned. I want you to grant me permission to put them through extended training because these candidates will make up our spy network in several occupied townships in France very soon."

Maurice looked down at the pictures in front of him. "They all seem so young. They'll be at great risk, Vera. How do you propose we get them into their positions? Drop them by parachute like we do with our commandos and other agents?"

Vera nodded her head. "These women are going to be fully trained as SOE agents, and that will include all the necessary escape and evasion that might be required, should their circuits be compromised. I'm going to train them to be deadly, but I need your authorization to do so."

Maurice nodded his head. "Then you have it. Proceed with your plans. Now I have something to tell you," he replied.

Vera raised her eyebrows and listened attentively as the morning sun sent beams of light through his only window. "Okay, what is it?"

Her boss stood up, took his blazer from the coat rack. As he put his first arm into one of the sleeves, he spoke up. "I received a visit this morning from downstairs, and they've told me that they want to send the bombers in for the second mission to hit the underground base in Germany. They don't think the 5th SAS unit got into the base after the first bombing run, and they want to go ahead with the second one that they'd planned for. So, that's being organized right now. They told me that we'd be informed about the timing shortly, but they want to have another go at it. They think their bombs had an effect and want to try some bigger ones is what they explained to me. It would be a heck of a diversion, and Lieutenant Colonel Plante and his merry men can sneak their way inside without being noticed . . . hopefully. That's what they're thinking."

Vera was upset by the news. "Those men are all we have right now to help support the resistance in France and Belgium. If we lose the commanding officer or any of his men, then we won't be able to help these women get into positions in the townships in France. That would compromise all the work we're doing to help that country out of its current Nazi occupation. Have you given any thought to that, Maurice?"

Maurice opened the door to his office and looked back at his second in command. "They're looking at the bigger picture here, Vera, and we didn't send in a great deal of that unit because the majority of them were being used on missions elsewhere. That's why we had to use the Royal Marines to support them. If they can find advanced technology underground at that Nazi mountain base in Germany, we could reengineer what they find and we'd have an equal playing field with the enemy we're fighting. Perhaps we'll even make new things that could help us quash Hitler's plans for world domination! Let's go to the meeting and see what they have to say on the matter, shall we? Vera quickly reached out and picked up her pictures. She placed them back in the manila folder and walked out of the office behind him.

In the downstairs briefing room a short time later, Vera looked at her watch, sitting a few rows from the front. It was just before 9:30 a.m. Maurice sat himself down after shaking hands with several people who said hello to him. Vera looked around and saw familiar faces too. By her count, there were only eight people in the room. Then, she focused her attention back on her manila folder and started reading the written material behind the pictures that she had shown Maurice upstairs in his office. There were details about an SS officer who had been working at a secret factory in France. They'd finally been told a name thanks to the white mouse and the intelligence she'd been able to relay back to F-Section in London, and Vera was still trying to learn more about who he was and why he was in France.

At 9:35, Ian Levington, a middle-aged man, came into the room and stood at a podium in front of everyone. He was missing an ear, which had been burned off of the side of his face back in World War I. He must have suffered greatly, Vera thought, Levington started the briefing.

"Good morning ladies and gentlemen. Thank you for coming to our meeting. Today I'm here to provide you with some details about Operation Grapefruit," he said as he looked around and smiled at Vera and Maurice. "A few days ago, we launched an air-sea-land operation that dropped new types of deep-penetrating energy wave bombs that we believed would help us destroy German bunkers. Our target was a suspected underground mountain base inside the German countryside that is close to the borders of Belgium and the Netherlands.

"We sent in a lot of bombers, and only a handful were able to return, I'm sad to report. Additionally, we deployed land forces, which were inserted by submarine drop off as well as through long-distance travel by collapsible boat. They were Special Forces, but they encountered rough seas, and I'm amazed that they even made it to the German coastline, but we believe they did, though not at the right time, unfortunately. Specifically, I'm talking about the Royal Marine Commandos and the newly created 5th Special Air Service Regiment. Their commander has volunteered to take the unit out on this mission," he told his audience who listened attentively.

Maurice coughed and apologized for disrupting the briefing. Then, Agent Levington continued. "We have been receiving reports for some time that Germany has been using slave labour to build underground facilities in occupied countries such as Poland, France, and other parts of Europe. The theory going around is that the Germans are trying to make super weapons including but not limited to a nuclear possibility in underground factories. We hardly know anything about these places, but word on the ground in France is that slave labour is being used. We have received valuable information from F-Section, and I thank Maurice Buckmaster and Vera Atkins for running such a proficient group of operatives. The information that they have been able to pass on has been extremely helpful."

Vera smiled at the acknowledgement and was thankful that F-section's hard work had just been acknowledged, but she was still worried about what this all meant as she continued to listen until Agent Levington asked her to comment about what F-section had turned up as far as recent intelligence went. Maurice asked Vera to say something on their behalf, and so she stood up and started telling everyone in the room what she knew. "People are being shipped by train all over the place to help Hitler expand his railways across Europe. If the Third Reich were to make a nuclear bomb that was mixed with the designs of the V2 rocket, they could strap it on a train and move it wherever they wanted," she said.

Ian Levington nodded and then added something else. "Thanks to the partisans and the escaped prisoners that have been extracted from occupied countries, we now know that the Germans have made several industrial-size underground factories where they are believed to be designing and manufacturing things of all sorts. Recently, information has come to light that pinpoints one of those underground factories—one that's below a solid granite mountain right on the border in the German countryside—but there is also something else I wish to convey to you about what kind of things the Germans are developing," he warned.

"From this last mission, we have also learned through the reports from many pilots, crew members, and fishing trawlers that are watching the coastline for us that the Nazis have a flying technology that we have never seen before. The aircrews have reported seeing flying orbs of light that move at great speeds and impossible angles as they harass our bombers. They've been given the name 'foo fighters.' They were so effective that they prevented many of our bombers from dropping their payloads on target, and they caused quite a few of our aircraft to crash into one another. It's been reported that the Germans have dozens of spherical orbs of light darting about in the night's sky at speeds that conventional aircraft are unable to achieve. The bottom line is that we don't know what these things are, but it's safe to say that they are manmade," he explained to them all.

As Vera and the others listened to Agent Levington, he continued with his briefing by saying, "The Nazi's have created some kind of luminous craft that can take our planes down with tremendous success. If we don't find out what they are or what the Germans are building underground, then we're in big trouble. We could end up losing the war. That's how serious this is. And so that's why we've decided to launch a second mission in the coming days, and hopefully, we'll be hearing more on whether or not our teams got into their base during all this chaos we're creating for them. Is there anything else you'd like to add, Ms Atkins or Maurice?" Levington asked.

Vera Atkins again stood up. "We have a name for the SS officer put in charge of these special operations in France. We didn't expect him to be at this particular base when we called in the air strike, but—who knows—he might have been. Whatever the case, his name is Captain Vunderbane. For all we know, he might already be dead, but if he wasn't killed in the first bombing mission, we want this man taken out as soon as possible, so let your people know what he looks like. I have a picture that I will pass over to you, Mr

Levington. Here it is," she said as she took out a picture and held it up for all to see. The image was of a handsome blonde man who appeared to be in his early forties.

"What do we know about this man, Vera?" Maurice asked her as he raised his hand slightly, indicating he wanted to interject and ask a question.

She looked towards her boss and answered. "He's a civil engineer and was well regarded for the projects that he worked on for Hitler before being appointed to his position. Our agents in France have told us that he sometimes travels between France and Belgium. We're working on a theory that there may be a U-boat base on the coastline of occupied France somewhere, but we haven't obtained confirmation of this yet, sir. That's all I can tell you right now," she said.

Ian Levington walked over and took the picture from her so he could have a copy made later. "Thank you, Vera. Your information has been most helpful. Now, if I might brief you on another matter that involves the United States Navy down in the Southern Hemisphere. As you know, they've been pushing back against the Japanese invasion of the South China Sea with a major offensive using the US Navy and their Marines. They've agreed to work with us if we share our information with them, and that is something that I would encourage us to do to some degree. We have reason to believe that the Nazis, under the careful planning of the Commander of the Navy, Karl Dönitz, might be moving cargo to occupied countries and perhaps even working directly with the Japanese—based on things we discovered over in Papua New Guinea just a few months ago," he stated. Then, remembering that Maurice wanted to say something, he looked his way and gave him the floor.

Maurice stood up and said, "Thank you, Mr Levington. I'm just worried that we don't have enough resources to help Belgium and France right now. If this Captain Vunderbane is from the SS, then he has the resources to build things, and that means troops, equipment, endless building supplies, and potentially a lot of slave labour. How do we fight that when we have such a limited amount of manpower on the ground? Adding to what you're telling us, the Nazis are now working internationally with their own allies. They're experts in designing and manufacturing things, and that worries me a great deal," Maurice stated and then sat back down.

"I can see the writing on the wall here, so let me just repeat that it's in our best interest to have the Americans continue to patrol the Pacific in the southern hemisphere while we continue to operate our observation posts on the many islands out there. It's only a matter of time before we discover what they're up to. Until then, please keep your nose to the grindstone and help us learn what the Nazis are making in these underground facilities. I hear your concerns, Maurice, and that's why we're boosting the number of Special Forces that will be working with the resistance in both France and Belgium, and they'll be more of them being inserted into occupied countries over the coming months, I promise you. We'll be organizing more supply drops to support the resistance forces too. Trust me, it's all in the works. Now I'll end this briefing by asking if there are any other questions or things that any of you would like to bring up . . ."

At the same time, the questions were being asked in that meeting room in London, Lieutenant Colonel Plante's SAS patrol continued towards the mountain that had been bombed and was still burning as the morning light began to increase all around them. As they approached a clearing made up of rocky outcroppings, they could see more of the damage from all the bombs that had been dropped on March 26.

They travelled light so that they could move around easier, but the climb was nonetheless a workout. The smell of burnt wood permeated through the trees as they came into areas where bombs had ignited parts of the forest. There were still many spot fires burning across the impact craters where bombs had fallen. Trees were entangled with each other. The place was a mess.

Corporal. Babcock was the first one to see the unexploded bunker-buster bomb that was stuck in the ground only thirty feet away from where they were. He pointed to it and got everyone's attention. It was passed down via hand signals to the last man of the group that there was an obstacle up ahead, so the patrol moved back into the treeline for a while. If that bomb went off while they were around, nobody would survive due to the concussion wave that it would give off a second after the detonation had occurred.

Carl was more than happy to continue forwards through the forest after that close call as the lead scout in their group. He heard a snap of some fingers from behind him and stopped after he climbed over a fallen tree. Lieutenant Colonel Plante had stopped and was showing the first man of the Royal Marines the unexploded ordinance that was so close to their present position.

He showed the major the bunker buster and the senior officer, then told his sergeant to bring each commando forward one at a time. A message was then passed on from soldier to soldier until every commando understood what was ahead of them and why they were changing routes so suddenly.

A few minutes later, Babcock was given the hand signal to continue ahead, and he started moving forwards again while assessing the environment all around him. It almost felt like it was going to snow as he looked up to the sky for a moment. As Carl moved through the forest slowly and cautiously, his eyes searched for signs of any kind of movement in his peripheral vision—just as he'd been taught while he maintained his cycles of combat breathing so his brain would have enough oxygen to react and be able to make the right decisions if the shit hit the fan.

By nightfall, the SAS commander had his large group of men positioned in several places a bit closer to the hidden airfield. They all knew that the second bombing run was expected on the night of April 1, so they had some time to observe the area and try to determine where the secret entrances were to access the tunnels that led to the underground base that they knew was there.

Chapter 7

On April 2 at a British Air Force base east of Suffield, Sergeant McClusky was working hard with Corporal Dailford as they tested one of the engines that they'd removed from a Lancaster bomber to rebuild. They'd been working on it all morning and believed they had finally figured out what the issue with it was. "This thing has been non-stop problems! I wish we could just put in a new engine and be done with the bloody thing," said McClusky, having become extremely frustrated with the job at hand.

Major Scott, who was the lead pilot of the Lancaster bomber that the two mechanics were working on, had overheard him as he walked into the repair hangar. "I'd rather have a new engine too if that thing is going to give me more problems in the air. We've just got our mission and it's over Germany, Sergeant. I guess we're short on engines. How's it going?"

McClusky looked over at the major and wiped his greasy hands on a rag while Dailford looked for something in his nearby toolbox. "With all due respect, sir, this bomber has been a right pain in the ass the entire time we've been working on it. This thing was so shot up from the German eighty-eights, it's a wonder it can still fly!"

Walking underneath his plane, Major Scott looked it over and saw the metal patchwork that had been finished on the underside of the main body. "You guys have put in a lot of man-hours into this aircraft! When I last saw the thing, it had holes all over it. It was a miracle that we were able to land it in one piece. The mission leaves in thirty-six hours. Can you have that engine back in place by then?"

Tom McClusky began walking away from the plane and exited the hangar with the major walking beside him. "We don't have a choice, do we, sir? Orders are orders, and I've been ordered to bring this thing back to life. You want to join me for a quick smoke break? My nerves are about shot, so I'm taking a moment for myself. Hey, Dailford, take a break as soon as you're done with the new spark plugs, mate. Get a coffee or something," the sergeant said as he looked back at the hard-working corporal.

"Thanks, Sergeant. I'll be another five minutes, and then I'll have one," he replied as he looked for another wrench.

Major Scott walked out with sergeant McClusky, and they stood outside the hangar and saw that clouds were coming. "There's a storm coming, sir. Might be bad weather for you over the ocean. You have your own smokes or do you want one of mine?"

Major Scott reached into his coat pocket and pulled out a cigarette container. He pulled out two cigarettes and offered one to the senior mechanic. Scott then pulled out a lighter and offered the sergeant a light.

Sergeant McClusky looked out over the multitude of Lancaster bombers that were being readied for the next mission, which was only a short time away. There were at least twenty planes that were in their close vicinity with crew and mechanics working on every single one of them as they tested out every system before each plane was sent up in the air. As the senior pilot exhaled a lungful of smoke, he looked back into the hangar at his plane.

Sergeant McClusky looked at the British pilot. He didn't envy him at all after he'd been forced to clean up the mess in the cockpit from the previous mission. He'd assumed the blood and guts had come from his co-pilot but had never gotten around to having that dark conversation. "We're going to be working on your plane around the clock, sir. The squadron commander gave us the order to fix as many planes as was humanly possible. The anti-aircraft fire that you received on the last mission completely decimated your internal communication and navigation systems so we have to start over and put in an entirely new wiring system on top of a pile of other things, including the hydraulics for the landing gear to work properly. That's what the next crew will be doing after we get that engine in the plane," he told the major as he sat down on the grass.

Major Scott joined him. Together they watched the beehive of activity before them as all ranks moved around the tarmac, poking their heads into every nook and cranny of their aircraft. Scott looked over at his plane's mechanic. "My nerves are still shot from the last mission, which was over a small industrial town in the Netherlands. I lost a good friend as well as both of my gunners at the mid-section and the end of my plane."

There was silence for a few seconds as McClusky tried to think of something to say. "We lost a lot of planes on that last one over Belgium, sir. A lot of good crews too," he started saying.

Major Scott took a drag of his fag and thought about his dead co-pilot. "I have to meet my new co-pilot in an hour in the officer's ranks. There's always the question of whether or not you can work with somebody new, especially on a mission over Germany. There's no time to really get to know somebody within that short amount of time," he replied.

McClusky looked at the pilot and nodded in agreement. "Plus, you have to get to know if your gunner's any good. No time to test them out either. I hope they know what they're doing for the rest of the crew's sake. It'll be sink or swim. So, you weren't on the last mission over Germany I take it?"

Scott shook his head. "Nope, and I'm not looking forward to this one. It's double the distance of my last mission. I'm a ball of nerves right now." McClusky heard the fear in his voice. "Sir, if it's okay with you, I'm going to suggest something. You got a girlfriend? Every pilot has a girlfriend or a wife, though you look too young to be married," the sergeant joked.

"Not married. No," he replied as he looked at the clouds that were coming towards them. "You can't do much on your plane tonight, sir, since my guys and I are working on it. So my suggestion is you take your co-pilot out for a drink in Nottingham and meet up with your girlfriend. Have a good time. Spend some time with her tonight and come back in the morning first thing. By then, I should have most of this baby overhauled. At least get a few hours getting to know your co-pilot over a few drinks."

Major Scott nodded his head. He thought about the idea and liked it. It made sense, and if he was going to be shot down within the next 48 hours, he needed to get laid before he died. He finally smiled at the senior mechanic. Sergeant McClusky knew he had connected with the twenty-seven-year-old pilot.

"Sergeant, that's the best idea I've heard since I got back. That's just what I'm going to do tonight," he said as he put out his cigarette and stood back up. He walked over to the butt can and put what was left of his smoke into it. As he did, he felt a few raindrops hit the top of his head, so he looked up above him and saw a wall of purple clouds. McClusky followed his lead and put his finished cigarette into the receptacle too.

At 1900 hours that evening, Major Scott and his new co-pilot Lieutenant Mike Saunders were walking down a street in Suffield. Saunders knew the area and saw the pub that they would be dropping into first. "It's over there," he said, pointing. As the two men crossed the street, they walked up to the entrance and went inside the three-hundred-year-old tavern.

There were quite a few people in the pub, many of them from the British Air Force. Major Scott looked around and didn't see his girlfriend, so he proceeded to walk up to the bartender and ordered two pints of beer for himself and his co-pilot. "I'll get the first round," he said as he smiled at his sidekick, who nodded back at him in appreciation. "That's a very nice gesture, sir. I'll get the next round then," the young airman replied.

After finding a table, the two pilots sat down and made a toast that their plane was functioning and would work without problems. "I'll drink to that," said Saunders. "This is my first mission in a Lancaster," he added nervously. He then took his pint and brought it to his mouth and tasted the beer. It had a slightly dark flavour to it.

Major Scott put his pint back on the table and took the opportunity to talk about the lieutenant's flight history because he had only glazed over the personnel files he'd been given before he'd gone back to his quarters to get ready for the evening's plans. "I know that this isn't your first bombing mission, though. You flew other types of aircraft last year from what I read in your personnel file."

Saunders nodded his head. "Yes, I did, sir. I flew in a Halifax BVII long-range bomber out of the 603rd bomber squadron. We completed fifteen missions, and then we were shot down. Several were captured and taken as prisoners of war. The pilot, Major Jeffries, ordered us to bail out over the ocean, and he stayed with the plane, which I watched crash into the sea. He didn't survive. Being in the water like that was one of the scariest moments of my life. The ones who bailed out first did so over land, but I was arguing that I should stay with the major, though in the end, he ordered me to go. I still have a lot of survivor's guilt over that one. I was the only one to make it back to England."

Intrigued, Major Scott asked him another question. "Did somebody come to your rescue? Was this during the day or the night?"

Saunders finished another sip of his beer and then put it down on the table in front of him. "We were on a distraction mission over France. British Intelligence wanted to fool the Nazis into thinking we were bombing industrial targets when, in fact, the real reason—I heard through the grapevine—was to insert spies into different areas, so they made us do the run in the daytime. We lost quite a few planes as a result. A lot of good crew too, so I hope it was worth it. I got picked out of the sea by a fishing trawler. They saved my life and took me to England. I'm forever in their debt.

At 2000 hours, Henry noticed his girlfriend enter the pub with two of her girlfriends. They all looked very attractive. He looked over at Mike and made a suggestion. "Okay, they've arrived. Let's not talk mission-related stuff at all, and please don't call me sir anymore. We're postponing military rank until tomorrow morning. I'm going to call you Mike and you're going to call me Henry. I don't know which of Laurel's girlfriends is interested in you yet, but just play it cool and watch how they communicate. I know she said she would find somebody that was interested in dating a pilot."

Mike picked up his pint and took another sip of it before replying. "Okay, we have a plan then?" Henry raised his hand to grab his girlfriend's attention. She saw him a few moments later and walked towards their table. "Yeah, don't say very much and let them do the talking," he said with a laugh.

Laurel walked up to Henry, ducked into his outstretched arm, and bent forwards to kiss him. "Hello, mister. How are you?" she asked, smiling.

Henry smiled back into her beautiful blue eyes as he looked at how well dressed she was. "I'm fine. How are you, ladies?"

Laurel stayed beside Henry and introduced her friends. "This is Katie and Margaret." Mike and Henry both said hello, and then Mike introduced himself. He offered to go and get the ladies some drinks, but Laurel declined the offer. "I promised the girls I'd buy the first round, so give me a moment and I'll be right back. She then kissed Henry again, and Mike could see that Henry was grinning from ear to ear.

"This place is starting to fill up," Katie said to Margaret. Mike looked around and saw that this was, indeed, the case. He wasn't sure why, though. "This pub doesn't normally fill up in the middle of the week. It's a bit unusual," Henry responded as he looked around the old pub and saw people in every direction.

"That's because there's a dance happening tonight, and we've been shut in for some time. I think the whole town is going," Margaret said as she took off her coat and put it over the back of her chair. "Ah, that explains it. That's why all of you ladies are dressed so nicely. I take it that's where Laurel wants to go?" Henry asked as he took out his cigarette holder and offered a cigarette to each of the ladies. Katie accepted and took one, but Margaret didn't care to smoke, so Henry helped himself, then offered one to Mike.

"Don't you like to dance, Henry?" Katie asked with a smile.

"Sure I do, but I don't get the opportunity to get out very much. When is the last time you were able to get away from things and have a bit of fun?" Henry asked in response to Katie's question. "Not very often. That's why so many girls are in this pub right now. Look around you," she said jokingly.

A few minutes later, Laurel returned with three gin and tonics. Everyone seemed to be getting on well. They talked for some time and decided to have a game of darts, but at 8:45 p.m., the ladies wanted to move on to get to the dance, which was being held at a community hall.

After they paid their entry fee and went inside, they could hear the band playing as they checked their coats in. It was a good thing that they'd come early because there were already at least one hundred people dancing and having a good time. Henry looked around but couldn't see a table to sit down at. He saw that every window had blankets over it so no light would be allowed to escape out into the streets, but Margaret saw one and pointed it out to Laurel, so the group moved over towards it but had to carefully move through many people who were either dancing or watching the band play while they drank and smoked.

The place was lively, and people were dancing and having a great time until 11:30 that night. Then, some army personnel got into a heated argument with some air force pilots. First, it started with pushing, and then things started to quickly snowball. A screaming match ensued, and finally, punches started flying in all directions. It was pure bedlam. Henry saw the writing on the wall as security for the dance started moving towards the brawl at the edge of the dance floor. "We'd better get the hell out of here or we may well wind up back at base in a jail cell!" Henry said to Laurel.

Laurel was worried. "What about our coats that are in the coat check?" She asked as she looked at how fast the fight was spreading out onto the dance floor. There were now dozens of young men throwing punches at each other.

The band stopped and the lights went on. "Forget the bloody coats! Let's get out of here! We'll come back for them tomorrow," Laurel stated emphatically as she saw the danger of getting crushed by so many people wanting to get away from those still fighting. As they moved towards one of the exits, a bunch of people got pushed backwards, toppling over Margaret and Laurel, but thankfully Mike and Henry quickly rescued them.

It was hard to get by people as they tried to recover from falling over, but they managed. Somebody started blowing a whistle, which meant the military police, had shown up. They'd made a good decision, and having emerged, they soon saw that there were already many people outside the community hall looking for another party to go to.

As the group walked up the street away from the dance hall, Katie mentioned that it was quite cold with no jacket on and asked, "what are we going to do now?" Laurel immediately suggested that they give up looking for another pub and instead go back to her flat because her roommate was gone for a week and she still had a few bottles tucked away from their last adventure. Margaret laughed because she remembered their last party there. She'd met a pilot and they'd fooled around on the couch after everyone had either passed out or gone to bed. She'd really fancied him but had lost contact—to her regret. She didn't know if he was alive, dead, or had simply moved on to another girl.

As they walked down the cobblestone road, they crossed over to the other side of the street and began walking out of the large town. There were many buildings along the way, but none of them showed any light emanating from inside because every window was covered with something due to there being a blackout through the entire area.

Back at Laurels place, the festivities continued. Laurel came out of her room and showed everyone in the living room that she had vodka and gin to offer people. Katie asked for another gin and tonic and got off of the couch and went into the kitchen to get some glasses. She looked back at Mike and asked him if he'd like a drink. He nodded and replied, 'Whatever your having is fine with me. Can we smoke in here or would you prefer if we went outside?"

Laurel looked at Mike and said, "You can smoke in here, but before you do, how about you get the music going? The radio is over there, and it's working. Find us a station that has some music. If you can't find anything, I have some albums that we can play on the phonograph."

Mike got up from the couch and walked over to the radio. He looked over at Margaret, who was already looking at the recordings that Laurel had. There were several that interested her. "Would you mind if I played one of these? I wanted to hear this one the last time we had a party, but I wasn't in a good state the last time I was here and I missed the opportunity to listen to it," she said.

Several minutes later, the music was going and the ambience inside Laurel's flat became quite enjoyable for all concerned. By 1 a.m., however, Katie and Mike had gone into the spare room and shut the door behind them. Margaret was in the bathroom vomiting from drinking a few too many gin and tonics, and Laurel and Henry were in her room having some incredible sex.

When Margaret came out from the bathroom, she could hear the sounds of passion emanating from both bedrooms. She drank some water in the kitchen and listened for a few moments. She went to the phonograph and put on another recording but kept the volume on low as she laid down on the chesterfield and put a blanket over herself as she contemplated whether or not she'd go in to work the following morning at the factory.

At 5 a.m., the alarm in Laurel's bedroom went off, waking Henry out of a deeply relaxed state. When he woke up, he was still drunk. He reached behind him and felt the lovely ass that Laurel had over the top of a sheet. He then rolled out of the bed and fell to the floor, which woke him up. He stood up slowly and looked at his girlfriend. He hoped he would see her again. He wanted to.

After opening the bedroom door and walking out into the darkened hallway, he heard some music and wondered who was still up. As he walked out into the living room, he saw that Margaret was alone and asleep on the couch. He continued into the bathroom and immediately smelled the vomit that was on the floor beside the toilet. He avoided stepping in it and relieved himself. When he was done, he flushed the toilet, washed his hands and threw some water on his face to wake himself up some more.

A knock on the bedroom door where Mike and Katie were sleeping had no effect, so Henry knocked on the door a second time a bit harder. When he heard no response, he tried the doorknob and turned it so he could enter the bedroom. As soon as he was inside, he could smell the passion lingering in the air. "Hey Mike, it's time to get up. We have to go, mate," Henry said to his friend, as he looked at the couple asleep on the bed in front of him.

All he heard in the semi-darkness was a grunt, so Henry tried again, but this time walked over to the side of the bed that Mike was sleeping on. He touched Mike's arm and that woke him up straight away.

"Mike, it's time to go. Get up. Have a shower. Get dressed. I'm going back to the bathroom to have a shower myself. Are you awake?" Henry asked just to make sure Saunders was going to get out of bed.

"What time is it?" Mike asked as he rubbed his eyes. He was still feeling drunk and didn't know if he could manage to walk to the bathroom without stumbling. "It's just after five in the morning. We need to get a move on, mate. The party's over, I'm afraid. Time to get back to base. You hear me? It's time to go to work," Henry said firmly.

Mike opened his eyes and took in a deep breath as Katie woke up and started moving under the sheets. "Okay. I'm getting up. You go on and have your shower, mate. I'll come out as soon as I hear you knock on this door again, OK?"

Satisfied that Saunders was awake and would get up on his own Henry left the bedroom and went back to the bathroom. Margaret was asleep but he tried to walk quietly so as to not wake her up. When he was inside the bathroom again, he turned the shower on and got in. The cold water woke him up straight away.

Five minutes later, he was out of the shower. He dried himself off and then put on his clothes. He walked out of the bathroom and went back to the other bedroom. At first, he thought he was hearing things coming from inside the room, but he didn't think much about what he was hearing since he had water in his ears. When he opened the door, however, he saw Katie on top of Mike having one last go at it. Suddenly, Katie realized that somebody else was in the room and she yelled with fright and jumped off of Saunders' torso and went under the sheets—but- not before revealing her beautiful body to Henry.

"Good morning," he said joyfully as he smiled at her.

Katie was not impressed. "Don't you know how to knock Henry?" she asked as she leaned back against the pillows on her side of the bed.

"I actually did knock, but you two obviously didn't hear me. Anyways, I'm sorry for disturbing you two. I'll leave the room now, but Mike, we have to go. Get yourself into the shower now while I go and say goodbye to Laurel. I don't have time to babysit, so let's get moving."

Saunders nodded. "No problem. I'm getting up," he replied as Henry walked out of the room. Scott walked out of the bedroom and went across the living room floor and was soon back into Laurel's room where he kissed her and said sweet things until he couldn't stay any longer. They felt quite attracted to each other. She looked into his eyes and kissed him passionately. "Let's do this again," she suggested as Henry held her close.

At a quarter to six, the two pilots left the flat and walked down the street. They were unsure how they would get back to the base for their zero eight hundred timing that they'd been given. That was breakfast time followed by the officers' briefing for their mission. If they missed breakfast, it would still be okay, but they knew damn well that there would be hell to pay if they didn't show up for the O-group.

Soon, they were in front of the pub that they had been at the night before. It was closed, and there were no signs of life. There were no taxis around, so they looked for other methods of getting back to base. Saunders suggested that they walk back to the dance hall and see if there was any activity around that area. The major didn't have any other ideas, so that's what they did. They walked down the empty streets and soon saw several men sleeping in an alley. They were obviously military men judging by their short haircuts—poor souls who hadn't found any other place to go after the dance shut down the night before.

That gave Scott an idea. He suggested that they look for the military police, but when they didn't see any signs of them, Saunders suggested they put a call into base and tip them off to there being some drunk soldiers in the alleys near the dance hall and that these soldiers or airmen had no means of getting back to their bases wherever they might be. "That's a bloody good idea, Saunders," Scott said.

It didn't take long to find a phone booth. Major Scott made the call, and soon a transport was dispatched to get all the drunken servicemen and bring them back to base. They only had to wait for them to show up and then they'd catch a ride back without any punishment or being accused of being AWOL. While they waited, Henry cracked some jokes about walking in on Katie and Mike, but Saunders said the night was a moment in time he would cherish forever and complimented Henry for pulling it off. It had helped Mike and Henry distract themselves from the thoughts of the impending mission. Mike pulled out his cigarette holder and offered his commander a smoke.

At thirteen hundred hours that afternoon, Sergeant McClusky was standing in front of Major Scott's Lancaster bomber waiting for the two pilots to get to the cockpit to start checking things out on the inside of the plane. They'd been working all morning on the inspection of the exterior, and when Scott had given the senior mechanic the thumbs up, they climbed up inside at the back and worked their way forwards. As they walked from the rear gun turret, they looked at the new 12.7 mm machine guns that had been installed. They gave the bomber more firepower, which was appreciated greatly by the crew. Inside the rear turret, Corporal Hailey was making sure everything worked properly.

When Major Scott saw Hailey working hard, he moved forward with Lieutenant Saunders following behind him. Soon, they came to the upper-middle turret and saw the new senior gunner inspecting the seat of his turret. "How are things going for you, Sergeant?"

Sergeant Clark looked up at the major and said, "We're getting there, sir. The guns still need to be tested, though—whenever we get the chance."

The major stopped for a moment and looked at the patching job that McClusky's crew had done on the skin of the plane. They'd done a good job repairing the holes from the German fighters' bullets and the rips from the anti-aircraft rounds that had torn through the plane and killed his two gunners in a split-second. "We'll test them out once we get out over the sea. Have you got the ammunition for them yet?" the senior pilot asked as he looked back towards the cockpit.

"No, sir," he replied as he got out an oily rag and started wiping down the breech of one of his guns. "I'm going to go and sign for our ammunition in thirty minutes after I've inspected the other gunner's weapons."

The major looked towards the back of the plane and examined the other gunner in the very rear. His name was Corporal Reece. Then, he turned back and looked at Clark. "Very good, Sergeant. Make sure these guns are in working order because our lives depend on them working when we need them and I can assure you that on this mission, we will definitely be needing them to work properly! Stand by to test the internal communications. Headsets on. Give the order. Carry on," Scott ordered as he and Lieutenant Saunders continued up to the cockpit.

As the two pilots walked forwards, they saw the flight engineer and the navigator working over a small table, looking over maps of Germany and its coastline.

"Put on your headsets gentlemen. Let's test the new system," Scott ordered as he locked eyes with the wireless operator and the bomb aimer who were working at their stations nearby. "Put on your headsets. Let's get ready. Take your seats and buckle up. Make sure you're ready. I want to test the engines shortly. Stand by," he finished, walking by everyone and entering the cockpit. Behind them, they could hear Sergeant Clark giving the order to the other gunner to ready his headset and get ready for a test of the newly installed internal communication system.

After Major Scott sat down in his pilot's seat, Lieutenant Saunders did the same thing. They checked the instrument panel and then checked their seats because, on the last mission, the cockpit had sustained a lot of damage where the co-pilot sat. "Things look really patched up from where I sit," said Lieutenant Saunders as he put on his headset and hit a few switches on the console.

He adjusted his headset and then started talking. He called for all stations to report back on how they could hear him, and soon every person inside the aircraft had given their report. Outside, Sergeant McClusky looked on as he waited for some kind of a sign from Scott, and when he saw him giving him a thumbs up, he also gave a thumbs up and then walked back into the hangar to start working on another engine that needed to be overhauled.

"Sergeant McClusky seems pretty happy?" Major Scott said as he smiled and took off his headset.

Saunders watched him as he disappeared through the hangar doors. "That guy works miracles. Would you look at what his crews did to this plane? They brought this thing back to life. You said it was barely able to land, right?" he said, looking at the ceiling of the cockpit.

The major nodded as he adjusted his seat. "I couldn't believe we didn't explode when we landed. We were on fire and had to crash land with only two landing gear working—and three dead men on board. I only needed stitches on my right leg, so I got off easy. A few more inches my way, and I would have been killed too. It's hard for me to be in this thing. I'm still seeing faces of people that aren't here anymore," he replied in a saddened tone of voice as he tried not to think about what had happened on their last mission. Stand by for the engines. Let's start her up and see how they sound," said the major.

A few moments later, the first engine started, and soon enough, the other three were running loudly. Sergeant McClusky came out of his hangar with several of his crew members, and they patted each other on the back as Major Scott gave them all a salute for a job well done. McClusky responded with a thumbs up, and then he lit up a cigar to celebrate the moment.Several minutes went by, and then the major shut down the engines, satisfied that their plane would fly on the mission to Germany. Now that he knew the plane was functional, he ordered everyone out, so the 3–4000-pound bombs could be placed inside the large bomb bay compartment linked together. On this mission, there would be no bomb bay doors on their bomber or any of the others. Once that was completed, they would be ready for their takeoff time at 2300 hours.

Chapter 8

Corporal Babcock looked at his watch as he heard the cacophony of bomber engines belonging to what he thought must be hundreds of planes. They were overdue but better late than never. What he was hearing sounded like the heavens above him had ripped wide open, exposing the sounds of the universe for all to hear. His fellow soldiers couldn't see the planes, but they knew that they were fast approaching. "What time is it?" Sergeant Mitchell asked as he stopped looking up at the sky and turned to look towards his team to make sure everyone was ready to go. Carl looked back at him and replied, "It's 0329 hours exactly."

Suddenly, everyone was taken back when from within the forest in front of where a number of anti-aircraft guns announced themselves in great succession. One after the other, they fired their shells into the sky, hoping that the exploding rounds would hit one of the British bombers. The SAS commander was angry with himself because they hadn't spotted these German positions yet and they could easily take out the bombers that were on their way to drop their payloads on the side of the mountain where the secret underground base was situated.

"Shit! Where did they come from?" Plante asked Sergeant Mitchell, his second in command, as they stared towards the forest.

Mitchell shook his head, feeling like an idiot for not having seen them either. "We have to take them out, sir. Let me take a group into the woods, and we'll find them," he suggested. Plante agreed quickly. "Okay. Go and wipe them out, but Sergeant, in less than five minutes, those planes are going to be dropping their bombs and if we're topside we're going to feel those concussion waves! I'm moving our teams to the airstrip. I want you to meet us there in fifteen minutes. Pick your men and get moving!"

Sergeant Mitchell didn't waste any time. He took Corporal Babcock with him along with two others, and they all disappeared into the darkness of the forest in just a few minutes' time as the plane's engines grew louder and the German anti-aircraft guns continued their barrage into the sky above them.

It wasn't very long before the SAS commander could see the first wave of planes, which filled up the sky. They were Lancaster bombers. He couldn't tell how many there were exactly because many of them were hidden behind clouds, which would make finding their targets on the ground quite difficult for the bomb aimers on board. That might make things dangerous for any of the friendlies that were moving around on the ground, he concluded. The thought hit home as he heard the first wave drop their bombs. They made an eerie sound as they descended from the sky.

"Let's move. Bombs away! We have to get away from here quickly!" Plante ordered. He looked through his binos one last time and started waving frantically, hoping the Royal Marine commander would see him and get the message to clear out from where he was and head to the airstrip. Thankfully, the major shot back a red light flash, and the patrol commander then continued on his way with the men around him.

It was only a minute later when the first bombs made impact. Bright red fiery balls of light illuminated the darkness around them, and then the concussion blasts from the 4000-pound bombs pushed people down onto the ground with great force. Nobody could stay standing upright when those things detonated. It seemed like the ground was shaking and about to rip open and swallow everyone up. In awe, Corporal Babcock moved behind Mitchell, at the ready as he started his combat breathing technique and became hyper-aware of his surroundings.

In the forest, Sergeant Mitchell could see at least a dozen well-hidden anti-aircraft guns that had been brought in by truck and put into position. There were huge numbers of Germans in those woods, and they were all focused on firing their guns up into the sky, which allowed his team to get closer. He stopped his advance and called everyone into a quick all-around defence position. "Look here. I want everyone to crawl up to a position and toss as many grenades as you can at them. We're going to lob these things after the explosions from the bombs go off. I'll take the rear position and just keep going. When we're out of grenades, start shooting at the crews and make your way to the other end. If we get separated, make your way to the airstrip and look for Plante. Any questions?"

There were no questions. Each man readied himself and then moved out on his own as they headed towards an enemy anti-aircraft position. Suddenly, off in the distance, several more explosions from a Lancaster's payload hit the ground. The explosion was massive, and the concussion wave hit the Germans, knocking them senseless for a moment or two. Babcock was also given a nosebleed and pushed down flat. After wiping his nose, he pulled the pin on his first grenade and lobbed it through the darkness. Then, he ducked down into the shadows while the others from his attack force did the same thing.

Whumph! Whumph! Whumph! Whumph! Whumph! Whumph!

Six artillery guns were taken out by their grenades, but the SAS soldiers kept moving through the darkness. The Germans were either dead or screaming in agony from wounds sustained from the grenade explosions. Sergeant Mitchell let a grenade go from his outstretched hand, and as he reached another artillery piece, he threw a second grenade at one of the soldiers facing the other direction. It hit him square in the back, and he turned around to see what had fallen to the ground. By the time the German soldier focused on the grenade, it was too late, and he and his crew were killed after it detonated.

Within two minutes, eight anti-aircraft guns had been taken out. Lucky for the four-man Special Forces team, they saw each other and kept close together as they moved ahead swiftly. Soon, they were paired up and started sniping Germans who were shooting their weapons into the darkness while others were still manning the anti-aircraft guns as the Lancaster's continued to drop their bombs from above. The noise was so disruptive from all these explosions going off that it made communication extremely hard if not impossible between the German artillery crews.

Mitchell's team took full advantage of that chaos. By the light of the flashing bombs, they were able to fire their weapons and take out multiple targets while they were exposed to the tremendous fireballs caused by the British bombs that were now exploding in great numbers on the side of the mountain nearby. Soon, they were back up on their feet, moving towards their next targets, and hoping they could take them all out.

At the hidden Nazi airstrip, the Royal Marines had already started sniping out German soldier sentries. They had plans for their uniforms, so they were taking headshots when they could manage. While the major's commandos did their part, Lieutenant Colonel Plante and his SAS soldiers caused distractions, blowing up fuel dumps and planes to cause as much chaos as possible.

The Germans were running around like ants after their nest had been disturbed. People were shouting and screaming orders at each other, but while that was going on, Plante and several of his men were bringing down accurate fire from behind several trees as dozens of gigantic explosions from the aerial bombardment lit up the darkness.

As Sergeant Abbott waited near the secret stump entrance to the German underground tunnels, the forest where sergeant Mitchell and his attack force were taking out the anti-aircraft guns was suddenly hit with several enormous explosions from falling British bombs that had landed off target. Some of the second wave of Lancasters had released their bombs, and they'd gone off target and were now landing near the airstrip.

Even more explosions started ripping up the earth much closer to where they were. Trees were being shredded all around their hidden positions as they ducked and took shelter. Abbott was then joined by the major, who called for his men to come forward out of the forest near the stump entrance. They were dressed up as Germans and could easily have been mistaken for enemy soldiers, so the Royal Marine commander sent them down into the tunnel first. While doing so, Abbott looked around for Lieutenant Colonel Plante and saw him approaching with three other members of his SAS patrol.

Within several minutes of spotting Plante coming towards him in the illuminated darkness, the major realized that they'd suffered significant casualties. He was worried about the items that they'd recovered from the shot-down German plane—and whether or not they had enough manpower to venture down into the tunnels to discover what the Nazis had going on down there. He would have to bring this up with the SAS patrol commander.

Several more concussion blasts knocked down the commandos who were waiting for Plante's group to join them. Everyone around the major was in the prone position as large explosions illuminated the hidden airstrip. Several aircraft were now on fire, burning out of control, and there were mass German casualties everywhere one looked. There were no more active shooters because the Royal Marines had already taken them out.

Sergeant Abbott looked at Lieutenant Colonel Plante, whose face was covered in camouflage paint, and pointed to the forest where the other half of the SAS patrol had been sent to knock out the anti-aircraft positions. They'd obviously been effective because none were firing anymore up into the sky. "Sir, your other men are over there in those woods but many bombs landed in the area and they've not come out yet to re-join us."

Lieutenant Colonel Plante wasn't at all happy about the news, as bombs from the Lancasters continued to wreak havoc all over the area. The cloud cover just wasn't working in the favour of the British Air force that night. "We have to get underground now while the bombs are throwing the Germans off their senses," the major suggested to his commander, who listened attentively as he thought about the rest of his missing SAS team.

He looked into the eyes of the Royal Marine officer and asked him, "How many casualties has your platoon sustained, Major?"

Major Wilcock thought for a second and then replied, "Including the men we lost on the document recovery, we've lost almost half, sir, and your men in the woods haven't come out of it yet. What do you want to do?"

The patrol commander thought for several seconds. "We need to think about the documents too, but we have to move now if we're going down there. We'll leave a group on the surface and tell them to go up into the backcountry to the place where we planned to meet up after we left this area. If we're not back there within thirty-six hours, then they are to proceed to the Belgium coastline and get those documents and plans back to England somehow. So, pick three of your men and put them into sniping positions to cover this area for eight hours and ask them to watch out for the men that were sent into the forest over there. Get your men ready. I don't see them."

Wilcock smiled. "That's because they're already beneath us waiting for you. They're in German uniforms, and if you take your four men as they are, we can continue with your plan of you being POWs and my men acting as the Germans that are holding you prisoner. We'll act like we've caught you, and we'll ask where to find the commanding officer down there. Do you still want to go with that plan?"

Lieutenant Colonel Plante nodded. "I do. How's your German?"

Suddenly, more bombs exploded off in the distance. They were now landing back on target as the Lancaster's continued to drop their bombs. Seconds later, the men saw white balls of light shooting across the sky towards the bombers. Sergeant Abbott pointed up to the sky as he watched them move into the clouds and then out of them as they headed for the British planes. "Sir, there are the balls of light again. What *are* those things?"

Plante had no idea. He shrugged his shoulders. "Whatever they are, they're dangerous and we can't do anything about them. Let's go."

Twenty minutes later in the forest where the anti-aircraft guns were situated, Sergeant Mitchell was nudging Corporal Babcock with his combat boot to see if he was dead or not. Carl opened his eyes, expecting to see a German looking down at him, but there wasn't much he could do. He wasn't able to walk and could barely take in half breaths as he tried getting his lungs to work properly.

Mitchell saw Babcock open his eyes in the darkness surrounding them. "You dead yet?" he asked as he knelt beside the corporal to check on his condition. Off in the distance, more bombs were still falling from the sky and detonating. The red fiery light and the smell of burning trees were all around them. It seemed like they were in hell. Babcock could see Mitchell talking but couldn't hear him. There were loud ringing tones in his ears. He attempted to sit up, but his eyes started rolling around like he had some really bad vertigo, so he lay back down on the ground.

The sergeant suddenly heard German soldiers coming their way and prepared for the inevitable as he left Carl and hid in the prone position behind a tree just twelve feet away from where Carl was situated. As the two Germans got closer, they saw Carl's body and walked over to it, but then they were suddenly hit with several bullets and died instantly. Their bodies fell to the ground, but it took Carl several moments to realize that there were two dead Nazis lying beside him as he stayed still upon the cold and damp ground beneath a large cedar tree.

Once again, Sergeant Mitchell returned and tried to talk to the corporal. When he realized Carl was alive but was really out of it because of the concussion blasts from the bombs, he gave up talking to him and started dragging him by the feet so they could get out of there while slinging both of their rifles over his shoulders.

Underground several hundred yards away, the SAS commander was getting acclimated to moving his men forward in the upper tunnel system. Eight men wearing German army uniforms moved towards a stairway that went downwards to a lower level. The SAS team, who were now playing the role of captured prisoners of war, consisted of Lieutenant Colonel Plante, Corporal Oliver, Trooper Harris, and Trooper Martin.

As they came up to the archway encompassing the doorframe, they recognized a sign painted into the cement above it. Rather than sneak up to it, they marched like Germans would do within their own base. Further down the tunnel, they could see German soldiers cleaning up debris that had collapsed from the ceilings. Obviously, the bombs being dropped from the air were having a great effect on the first level.

Nobody seemed to notice them, so they continued down the stairway for two levels. They could have done more, but there were guards posted at a staircase below that, so they decided not to attract any further attention to themselves. Major Wilcock suggested that he duck out into the corridor and see what was going on. They could hear an alarm, and there were metal doors with painted numbers on them indicating what level they were at. As he opened the door, he cautiously looked around and didn't see anyone initially, but there were two directions that they could travel. He wasn't sure which one they should take, so he decided to grab two of his soldiers who were dressed as Germans and send them in one direction while he and another soldier walked in the other.

There were many metal doors on this level—all of which were locked and secure. The major tried to open several of them and wasn't able to get any of the door handles to open, so he gave up and came back to where the stairway was. A few minutes later, the other two soldiers came back and reported that there were quite a few Nazis working on something down the corridor that they had just gone down and some of them were trying to repair some of the cracks in the walls with slave labour being used to do all the hard work. This report was the first one that indicated that prisoners were being kept in these facilities. The men went back into the staircase and decided to try and bluff the guards that were below by telling them that they'd just captured some commandos and they were taking them to the senior officer of the base for interrogation.

Plante looked at the Major and once again asked, "is your German really that good, Major? Because you're going to have to have a conversation with them, and they'll be ready to shoot at us if they suspect you're not a legitimate Nazi soldier." The Royal Marine nodded his head and assured the SAS officer that he could do the job. "I speak German fluently sir. That's why they sent me on this mission with you."

Just in case, though, Wilcock told four of his men to hold silenced pistols behind their backs as they descended the stairs. When the two guards heard people coming they readied themselves and watched as the prisoners were brought down the stairs with their arms raised above their heads. The two guards wanted answers almost immediately and started screaming for everyone to stop right where they were on the stairs. Seeing that the stress was rising exponentially, the major stepped up and started talking to the guards.

Unfortunately, the German guards didn't believe the major and were about to fire their weapons, so the commandos opened up and shot the two guards dead. There was a blood trail starting to pool on the cement floor almost immediately, which could easily be seen, so the group quickly took to moving the bodies under the stairs out of view in a closet space that had been made beneath the stairs for storage needs.

Lieutenant Colonel Plante then assigned two of the commandos that were dressed up as Germans to replace the guards. Only one of them could understand German fluently, but for the moment, that's the best that they could do. There were no levels to go down, and now they had to find out what was on the other side of the metal door. The major opened it up and saw that there seemed to be a lot of wooden crates stacked in the hallways. They were obviously being moved from one place to the other out of several storage rooms.

As the group walked down the hallway, a German captain saw them and challenged them almost immediately. He wanted to know what they were doing down on the fourth floor, and that's when the major really shined. He gave the captain a Nazi salute and pretended to be a lieutenant from the airfield. Then, the major gave him an amazing story and pointed to the captured commandos. He explained that the British bombers had devastated the hidden airfield and that they had also been ambushed by British special forces but had been able to push them back and capture these men.

The German captain wanted to know why they were down there and why the guards at the door had let them inside. This was a level that required a high level of authorization to be in, and the guards should have known better than to let them enter. The major wasted no time and explained that the senior officer in the tunnels above them had been killed by debris from the ceilings and that he had been told to come down to the lower levels to report to one of the intelligence officers. He then asked the captain if he was one such person. The captain nodded, and then he contemplated his next move as he looked over at the captured prisoners.

The Nazi captain then waved his hand as he gestured for the lieutenant to follow him as he left what he was doing and took them down a tunnel that was big enough for a truck to drive down. As they walked by the crates that he was working on, everyone with an ounce of brain in their skulls could see shining gold bars packed in straw. They were amazed because there were hundreds of these crates stacked to the ceiling and there were eight other German soldiers moving the crates onto metal dollies that were designed to hold weight. The gold was being moved someplace else. The question was to where?

After walking down the hall, they came to a radio room, which had a radio operator and a phone with cables going through the walls into another room. The captain told the person he thought was a Nazi lieutenant to wait out in the hallway, and then he ducked in and used the phone. He made a report and received orders to bring them down to level four. The major was able to hear that much, and it meant that there was another stairway close by that would take them down into even deeper areas of the underground base. Wilcock quickly looked at his men at the back and told them to get their silenced pistols ready in case they were needed.

A few moments later, the captain came out and spoke to the lieutenant and told him that they were going to the lowest level where the admiral would see them with several intelligence officers wanting to be included in the briefing. It seemed as though the German officers were curious and wanted to have a first-hand report from somebody who had been on the surface when the British Bombers had unleashed their big attack. They wanted to know what kind of bombs they were using because they had been far more effective than the ones used on the previous attack. As the captain explained as much, a light flickered in the cement tunnel where they all stood.

Captain Otter was the intelligence officer's name. He took out his luger from his holster, walked over to the four prisoners of war, and looked at each of them. "You are commandos. Of that, I have no doubt. You have caused us many hardships, and you will pay for it dearly! Do I have to play a game with you and think that you do not speak German? They wouldn't send you on a mission into Germany without being able to speak the language, so understand that your lives are forfeit. The question is do you die slowly and painfully or do you get a bullet to the back of the brain so it's a quick death? Think about that before interrogation starts," he said to them in a fierce tone. Then, he looked over at the lieutenant and ordered him to follow him down the flight of stairs to the lower levels.

Before they started moving toward the stairs again, Wilcock took a quick glance at his watch. It was quarter to five in the morning. It would be daylight soon on the surface, and he hoped that the men he'd left behind were now safe and in hiding.

The German intelligence officer pointed down the staircase when they reached it. "Straight down to the bottom. Prisoners, keep your hands above your heads," he ordered as he watched Wilcock and his soldiers escort the prisoners down to the seventh level. The lights in the stairway were red, which created an eerie, almost hellish look.

As they came to a new level, they observed that there were guards posted at every door entrance, but the metal door was always shut, so nobody could see what was on the other side as they passed by each level, descending into the bowels of the base.

Finally, they came to a door that had the number seven painted on it, and there were more guards. Lieutenant Colonel Plante was thinking that the guards he had left back on the third level as guards must, by now, be pretty nervous, wondering where the rest of their party was and whether or not they'd ever be seen again.

Captain Otter suddenly barked an order to the guards standing beside the door that it be unlocked and that they be given access to the seventh floor. The sentries immediately moved into action and opened the door, revealing a massive underground complex with literally a hundred people moving around doing something important.

The German captain then took command as he held out his 9mm Luger and pointed it at the four prisoners. "Down there, towards the offices! Go!" He obviously didn't want anyone to see the enormous German U-boat that was moored to the side of the secret underground navy base. Everyone stared at it. This was not what they'd suspected to find down on level seven!

As Lieutenant Colonel Plante looked around, he saw many things that blew his mind. The gold was stacked in crates and was being loaded onto an enormous U-boat by a crane through the top deck while at least thirty gorgeous Slavic women were also being boarded onto the U-boat via a boarding ramp after at least a dozen men disappeared through the hatches at the top of it.

Over in a different area not far away from the U-boat, several soldiers were shouting orders at a dozen male slaves who were piling debris off in another corner. Major Wilcock surmised that this was coming from the damaged tunnel systems above them. They had to do something soon, as they saw dozens of German soldiers marching around, heading towards the enormous vessel.

Suddenly their heads turned towards the sound of a truck coming out of a tunnel. Fully loaded with large wooden crates, it made its way over to the extra-large U-boat and parked in front of it. Moments later, a second and a third truck came out of the tunnel that the first truck had come out from. They also made their way to the pier and parked. Then, a platoon of marching German soldiers approached the vehicles, and they started to unload the crates and pile them onto one side. Walking towards the admiral's office, the SAS commander studied the situation and realized that this

U-boat was getting ready to disembark and was going to be taking supplies somewhere important. It was time to cause chaos, and he started coughing to get everyone's attention.

Back on the surface, several Royal Marine Commandos were carrying Babcock on a stretcher that was made out of canvas and several branches from a fallen tree. Sergeant Mitchell was in the lead position in front of them while Corporal Tanner, another Royal Marine, was taking up the rear as they moved up into the mountains away from the totally destroyed airstrip.

As Sergeant Mitchell reached the top of a ridge fifteen minutes later, he looked down into the valley as the light of the new dawn exposed the carnage. Forest fires littered the countryside. The weather was frosty, which kept the ground wet and cold. As a result, the fires weren't expected to ravage the countryside, but even up where they were now, one couldn't escape the smell of the burning forest.

As the two commandos brought Babcock up onto the ridge, Sergeant Mitchell pointed to a spot where they could put him down and rest. When Carl was on the ground again, Mitchell went over to him to see how he was. "You still alive, Babcock? You'd better be because these guys will be mighty pissed off discovering that they were carrying a dead carcass all this way," he said.

Carl opened his eyes and was able to focus on his sergeant. "I'm still here. Can I try and sit up now? I'm breathing okay again, although I'm mighty sore from the concussion blasts. What kind of bombs were those things? They seemed way more powerful than the last ones," he commented.

Sergeant Mitchell looked over to the edge of the ridge and saw Corporal Tanner coming into view. "Take a rest, Tanner. You earned it," he said as he removed his water bottle and helped Babcock sit up slowly to take in some fluids. "It was too dark to see what kind they were, but they were way more powerful than the last ones. I agree with you there because I'm still having problems with my balance and hearing," he replied, smiling as he took out his canteen and offered it to Carl.

Corporal Babcock felt the muscles in his chest object to his moving around to adjust his position. He felt something in his mouth and was sure it was coagulated blood mixed with phlegm. He spat it out on a rock and watched it stick to the stone. "Yeah, I think I hurt myself pretty good, Sergeant. Thanks for saving my ass back there," he said as he accepted the canteen with his right hand and took a sip to rinse out his mouth. Seconds later, he spat out the water onto the ground beside him. He could feel the cuts his teeth had made on the inside of his cheeks. There were numerous cuts inside his mouth, and he was sure that several teeth were loose.

Carl suddenly realized that only sergeant Mitchell and himself had come out of the forest. "I don't remember walking out of the woods. What happened to Douglas and Spears?"

Sergeant Mitchell shook his head. "They didn't make it. I checked on them first, and then I found you, and you were still breathing, so I dragged you out," he replied sadly.

Shocked by the news that two of his friends had been killed ripped his heart in two. He remained silent and stared at Mitchell's face. Tears started forming in his eyes. Feeling overwhelmed, he leaned back against the rock face and just shook his head, still not saying anything. Sergeant Mitchell understood that Babcock needed some time to process what he'd just told him, so he stood up and walked over to the other three men to see how they were doing.

"What's the next leg going to be, Sergeant?" Corporal Tanner asked as he looked up at Sergeant Mitchell, who knelt down and took out his topographical map. "That's a bloody good question, mate. Let's take a look at this here map and see what the options are."

Chapter 9

On April 5, while at a depth of three hundred feet beneath the ocean, Corporal Mills alerted the executive officer of the British submarine HMS Seadog that he had a contact on his sonar. "Sir, we have torpedoes in the water! Bearing 132 degrees, approximately three miles away from our present location. I think it's a German U-boat, sir, that's fired the torpedoes. And where there's one, there's bound to be more of them. They have another target. I think they've discovered the Neptune, sir."

The executive officer, Lieutenant Hicks, gave the order to stop all engines and to let the submarine coast forwards in silence. They were hoping to get closer to the surface to make communication with the Special Forces that they'd inserted only twenty-four hours previous just off of the German coastline and the Neptune's job was to be available to help them by picking up any of the ground forces that needed to be taken out of there if it was required. This had been a scheduled event to offer the ground forces support if they needed it.

The sonar technician listened to one of the earphones that he had over his ear and listened as he heard the twirl of the props on each one of the torpedoes. Then, he heard the others being launched. "Sir, I hear another torpedo being fired from a different U-boat. Only, this one is closer to us. We're in serious trouble if there are more than two U-boats out there, sir. They're attacking their target from different positions."

"It's a bloody wolfpack. Damn!" replied the executive officer as he looked at one of his senior non-commissioned crew members. "Petty Officer McGill, go and get the commander, but do so very quietly. He'll want to know why I just shut off the engines."

"Yes, sir," McGill replied as he left the con and went to get the captain, but he only had to go part of the way because the commanding officer of the British submarine was already heading towards the con to find out what was going on. Petty officer McGill stopped and was about to explain when they both felt the underwater vibrations. A series of explosions had suddenly gone off some distance away from where they were situated. Then, they went down on to one knee and looked at each other, utterly shaken up by the event, as their sub shook from the concussion wave. "They got the Neptune, sir," the

Petty officer said sadly. The captain looked down and said nothing as they remained silent, listening to the twisting wreckage descend to the bottom of the ocean.

The British submarine wasn't able to send out a report back to London because they were on radio silence as soon as they'd entered German waters and they would surely be pinpointed if they were to send out any signals. Commander Biggs scratched his beard while he contemplated his options. The sounds that they were hearing came along with the hidden truth that many lives had just been lost. A minute later, he got back up on his feet and started walking towards the con. The petty officer followed behind him, not saying a word.

When the commander saw his executive officer, their eyes met. "Commander on deck," announced the XO. All hands in the area looked over and saw Biggs come into view.

Commander Biggs took command of the con and looked over at his sonar technician who was concentrating very hard as he listened to the Neptune crash into the ocean floor. "I'd like an update really quickly. Was that the Neptune that just went down?" The commander asked his executive officer. He didn't like seeing his second in command nod his head up and down.

Corporal Mills, the sonar technician, then looked up at Biggs and replied softly, "Sir, I can hear at least three German U-boats in the general area of the Neptune. They're making sure they sunk her, and they're not leaving the area until they're sure that she's out of the game."

In the galley, Major Babcock was trying to calm his nerves. He had poured himself a cup of coffee and was in the process of cleaning up the mess after it had spilled all over him following the explosion. He looked at the clock on the wall and saw that it was two in the morning.

The sergeant in charge of the kitchen walked over to him and handed him a rag to clean up his spill and tried to give him some assurance that the commander would be on top of this in no time flat. "Hang in there, sir. We're going to be okay. Can I get you another coffee or something else perhaps? You didn't eat yesterday. Are you okay?"

The major looked up at Sergeant Dunleavy. "Thanks for the cloth, sergeant. I'm not used to travelling on a submarine, but I'm glad that I'm here. Helps me understand more about what my son went through on the other side of the world," he replied.

Intrigued, Dunleavy asked him about his son. "Is he in the Navy or something sir?"

As Babcock wiped up the coffee that had spilled onto the table in front of him, he shook his head. "No. He escaped Singapore in February of forty-two on a small boat out into the open ocean. He was rescued at sea by a British Submarine and taken to Papua New Guinea. That's all I know . . ."

The senior believed the story and was quite impressed by the tale. "That would be one hell of an experience for anyone, sir. I'm glad that you got a ride in one of Her Majesty's tin cans then. It'll help the two of you understand each other a bit more after the war's over," he said as he offered the major a hand towel to clean his hands with.

The major nodded. "Thanks, Sergeant. Too right about that one. I'm glad neither of us joined the Navy. I don't think I could have done this kind of job full time—year in and year out. That takes a special type of personality, which I don't seem to have. I crave the air and the sky too much I think," the SOE operative replied as he started trying to wipe clean the clothing that had been stained by the coffee.

A day later, back in London, Vera Atkins looked up at the clock on the wall just as her intelligence officer entered her office to give her an update before she went to give Maurice Buckmaster his evening briefing. It was 1700 hours on April 6, so she had another half-hour before she had to leave her office to go over to his. Vera was disappointed that there was still no word from the fishing trawlers or the two British subs that were supporting Operation Grapefruit. "Why haven't we heard anything from any of them, Captain? Where should they be right now?" she asked curiously.

Armstrong hesitated for a second. "The subs were in the North Sea on patrol, heading in for a scheduled land-to-sea visual communication near the German-Netherland border, but we don't know if they got there or not yet. They're not supposed to make contact until 0100 hours on April 7. They need time to get to their rendezvous point, so they can make contact with ground forces by visual aid," the intelligence officer replied.

Vera responded thoughtfully. "The Germans know that we're onto them. They're angry that we attacked them on their own soil a second time. I can't help but feel nervous about this entire operation. I was thinking about submarine insertions into France for my circuits, but it may not be safe to use them if the Nazis have U-boats patrolling France and the Netherlands' coastlines. I'll have to rethink how I end up inserting more agents into France. Keep me informed of any updates, will you please, Captain?"

Armstrong nodded. "Of course, m'am. I'll inform you right away as soon as I hear of any updates for you," he replied and then left her office to go right back to the communication centre for F-Section. He was just as curious as she was. After Armstrong left her office, Vera's secretary came in to see if she wanted a cup of tea made, and when she responded affirmatively, she saw that the second in command of F-Section was staring at a map on the wall that showed Germany, the Netherlands, Belgium, and France in great detail.

"Would you like a cup of tea, Vera?" Margaret asked. Atkins looked over in her direction and smiled. "Yes, I think that's a good idea. I need to take a step back and see if I can do this next operation better," she replied to her helpful secretary.

Margaret could see that Vera was stressed. "It's overwhelming what's going on in France and Belgium right now, Ms Atkins—not to mention the worry about those bloody U-boats sinking so many of our merchant marine vessels. The Germans are hunting everything with their U-boats right now, it seems." While speaking, she walked over to the tea trolley that was sitting outside of Vera's office and started working on making her boss something to relax her nerves a little bit.

"You're right about everything you just said, Margaret. Thanks for making the tea," said Vera as she looked away from the map and went back to her desk to close the manila folders that contained profiles of the new agents she was planning on dropping into France very soon. "If they haven't made contact in the next 24 hours from any of our teams, then I'm going to have to consider this mission to be a failure," she said reluctantly. "I just hope that our Special Forces will recover if that's the case because I really need them in France."

Her secretary poured some hot tea and brought it over to her. "Don't give up on them yet, Ms Atkins. Our Special Forces are all over Europe. I know that much. They're often unable to send messages, and if they're anywhere on that map that you've been staring at, I'm sure Jerry's not going to be too happy about it. Meaning our lads are going to be running out of the hornets' nest after they blow up whatever they need to blow up, right?"

Vera nodded. "You're right. I need to give this more time. Have you sent off my request for the new agents I selected?"

Her secretary smiled as she was starting to walk out. "Yes, ma'am. It was sent out yesterday. I hope to hear something back soon from our training wing."

Vera smiled as she accepted a cup of tea, then walked to the other side of the trolley and helped herself to some sugar. "Excellent. That's a bit of good news," she said as she walked over to her desk and opened a drawer where she had a packet of cigarettes. She felt stressed and a bit overwhelmed, so while the tea in her cup cooled, she lit up a cigarette.

Her secretary then smiled at Vera and said, "I'll leave you to your work, ma'am," and walked out of her office.

Her boss smiled back at her and replied, "Thank you again, dear!"

Back in the Sea Dog, an engineering officer helped to get the torpedo fasteners secured so they could hold their payloads properly. The submarine was descending to the sea floor to hide from the U-boat wolfpack that they suspected was out there trying to hunt them down. Leading Seaman Gilbert was lying on a cot, trying to stay out of the way as the lieutenant moved around the torpedo room. The submarine creaked and groaned. Water continued to drip into the sub, but the teams kept the water pumping out. Lieutenant Shiles was inspecting the torpedoes and their support structure, looking for any faults with Corporal Hicks, who was one of the torpedo technicians.

Suddenly, they heard the captain's voice over the intercom: "Brace for impact. Brace for impact!"

Shiles knew they needed to move quickly and attempted to grab Hicks by his belt to yank him away from all of the torpedoes when the bow hit the soft sand on the sea floor. The lieutenant was instantly thrown forward, causing him to hit his mouth on the side of one of the torpedos. As a result, he lost several teeth, and to make matters worse, he bit through his tongue quite severely. The shock of the injury took his focus away as he fell to the floor in agony.

The corporal was on the ground too, but he'd been thrown backwards and hit his head on the hatch of one of the torpedo tube openings that they'd just been looking at, which was why it wasn't shut. The racks of the torpedoes were tremendously heavy, and Corporal Hicks held onto one of the vertical posts that made up the supporting structure for them. He'd needed to hold onto something. When he was able to stand back up, he saw how close they'd just come to their own deaths, when he saw that some of the racks had broken free from the walls of the sub. That was a real problem that would need fixing, but the lieutenant was hurt badly, and he chose to help him instead.

Hicks looked around, and started shouting for help. He was quickly heard, and several men ran back to shut him up when they saw what had happened to Lieutenant Shiles. One of them went onto the intercom and called for a medic to be sent down to the torpedo room right away.

Petty Officer McGill arrived ten minutes later and told them all to stay off of the intercom system. "We're on radio silence no matter what. Oh my God," he said as he suddenly observed all the blood coming out of Shiles' mouth while one of the crew members tried to assist him. "Did he bite off his tongue?" he asked Corporal Hicks who immediately shrugged his shoulders in response.

"I can't say for certain, PO, because there's so much blood coming out. We need to get him to the infirmary," he replied.

McGill went to get the doctor, and as he did, he helped several submariners get back up from off the floor as the vessel straightened itself out on the bottom. There had been a noise when the HMS Seadog dragged her belly across the sandy seabed. The commander wondered if they'd just made a fatal error. Had the U-boats patrolling nearby heard the noise too? He looked over at his second in command and said, "Get a report from all stations, please, but go and do it in person"

Lieutenant Hicks immediately repeated the orders. "Report, all stations. Aye-aye, sir. I'll send a runner since we're on radio silence."

Just then, Petty Officer McGill showed up and told the commander about Shiles and then let him know that he'd just sent the doctor to treat his injuries. When he explained that one of the torpedo racks had come loose, the senior officer looked quite concerned. He wondered if the torpedoes were safely stored or if they would fall off their racks.

The commanding officer thought for a second and then looked directly at McGill and said, "Stop by all stations and obtain a situation report. Get everyone onto making sure their stations are functional, and if they're not, I want to know about it," said the sub's commander as he looked over to his navigational officer.

"Right away, sir," the petty officer replied as he turned around and went back to do as he had been ordered. The executive officer then asked if he could go and check on the engine room and see if they needed an extra hand since they'd been having fuel pump issues.

The commander nodded. "Good idea. Keep them from making excess noise, and watch that nobody drops any tools onto the deck. They'll hear it," he whispered as Hicks left the con.

Biggs watched the XO leave the compartment and then walked over to his navigational officer, who was trying to get a fix on their present location. He walked by him and said, "I don't think you need to worry about us meeting our next timing, Lieutenant. We're not going anywhere," he said in a soft tone of voice as he looked at the map that the young officer was pouring over.

Continuing past the navigational officer, Biggs then approached his sonar technician. "I want you to keep me abreast of what you're hearing, Mills. I want everyone to slow down their breathing and focus on something that will help them relax. We're going to be here for a while, and we need to watch our oxygen consumption." With this, he looked down at the sonar equipment.

Corporal Mills looked at his commanding officer and said, "Yes, sir." He then put his headset back on and started listening attentively to what was going on in the ocean around them.

Chapter 10

At thirteen hundred hours on April 7, Corporal Babcock looked through his binos from his position on a rocky ridge midway up the side of a mountain that wasn't too far away from the coast. As he looked through the lenses, he tried to clarify if he had indeed spotted movement coming towards his group at the base of the mountain because he was on the lookout for the main patrol group led by Lieutenant Colonel Plante. He was doing his best to be useful while the others rested. What he saw was a group of men dressed as Nazis and three men in British fatigues. There were only seven men in total, which indicated that they had lost a great number from their original party.

Carl looked over to Sergeant Mitchell and called over to him in a low voice. "Sergeant, they're here," he said.

Mitchell immediately sat up and put his boots back on, and as he did, he asked Babcock for a report. "I'm only seeing a small number approaching as I look right to left. I'm making out four men in Nazi uniforms and three in ours. I can see Plante and Oliver, but Major Wilcock isn't with them. I'd say they had the fight of their lives down there."

Sergeant Mitchell looked over to the other two men, who were resting. "Get up, you two. They're here. Looks like we're going to have fewer men than we thought he'd have. We're going to have to hike out of here on foot, I'd say."

Lance Corporal Potter was packing up his gear nearby. He heard the conversation and looked over at Sergeant Mitchell. "What day is the scheduled communication with the submarine, Sergeant? Is that our method of extraction?"

Mitchell finished tying up his boot and then replied. "That was supposed to happen a few days ago, but we missed that window of opportunity. We'll see what the platoon commander wants to do, but it's one of two choices. Either we go into France or we go into Belgium. We'll soon find out either way, I guess. Let's get some water on the boil for them, Potter. They'll be hungry and tired. How you feeling, Babcock?"

Corporal Babcock looked over at Sergeant Mitchell and nodded. "Sore as hell, and I'm still leaking fluid out of one ear. I feel totally off balance when I walk, but I'm okay when I'm sitting or lying down like I am now," he said. "What about you?"

Sergeant Mitchell assessed his own injuries that he had sustained. He was sore, and like Babcock, his sense of balance wasn't working properly since being in the forest that was bombed. He had also suffered a bloody nose and was still hearing ringing tones in his ears. His pelvis was really sore—as were all of the joints in his body—and yet, somehow he still managed to get up and continue on. Now that all the adrenaline had left his body, however, he was feeling really tired and could have used several more hours of sleep.

"I'm sore as hell, but I'm doing better than those guys. They'll be exhausted. I want to let them rest up while we guard our position unless Plante wants to bug out of here. We'll wait to see what he wants to do next, but for the moment, I'm going to take Lance Corporal Smith down with me so we can guide them in," he replied as he moved over to where Carl was situated to have a better look.

By the time Sergeant Mitchell was able to meet up with Lieutenant Colonel Plante, it was closer to fifteen hundred hours. The SAS commander was pleased to see him standing in front of them with his arms crossed out in front of him in the shape of an X to signify that he wasn't a threat to their party. Plante stopped his patrol group and walked up to him. "It's so great to see you again, Sergeant. We've been on the move, constantly hoping we'd somehow find you alive and waiting for us."

Sergeant Mitchell uncrossed his arms and relaxed as the group of men went down onto one knee and covered their arcs of fire while the Platoon commander talked with the sergeant. "It's good to see you, sir, but what happened to the rest of the men?" he asked as he looked around.

The patrol commander shook his head sadly, then replied to his question as he accepted Mitchell's water bottle. "They're all dead. I can tell you about it when we get up to your position. Is it very far from where we are?"

Sergeant Mitchell shook his head and pointed up the mountain behind him. "No, sir. We're over by that rocky outcropping, so we could keep a look out for you. Babcock and Potter are up there getting some water on the boil for patrol.

Plante nodded in response. "We need to get out of here fast, Sergeant. Guess what's at the bottom of the underground base?"

Sergeant Mitchell shrugged his shoulders. "I don't know, sir. What did you find?" he asked curiously.

The SAS commander then smiled and said, "There's a bloody U-boat base underground that travels all the way back out to the coast. I couldn't believe it when we saw it, and the U-boat that was down there loading up was enormous. It was bigger than any drawing or photograph of a U-boat that I have ever seen in my life. It's got to be something new that London doesn't know about," replied the senior officer.

Mitchell was shocked. The last thing he'd expected to hear from his commanding officer was that they'd discovered a secret underground U-boat base. That was amazing to hear, and he contemplated their next move. "Then I guess we need to get out of here ASAP! Are your men up for continuing over the mountains in the condition that they're in? I have food and water being prepared up at the ORV. Let's get you all back up there, and you can rest and take care of yourselves first. I'd say it'll take an hour to climb up there sir," he said.

Plante nodded his head. "That's a good idea. We're exhausted. Let's go then, Sergeant. Lead the way," he replied as he signalled for the men he was with to continue forwards.

At sixteen hundred hours, Corporal Babcock looked over at Lance Corporal Potter and said, "Okay, I see them. They look buggered! Better put that stuff away and look busy," he said calmly.

Lance Corporal Potter looked up from where he was sitting behind a rock formation, reading through some of the material that had been recovered from the German plane. "Okay, I'll put this away and get the ration packs out, but from what I've been reading, the Germans are miles ahead of what we have. This stuff needs to get back to London, mate, the royal marine sniper replied.

By 1700 hours, the SAS commander was enjoying a cup of coffee as he talked to Sergeant Mitchell a short distance away from the other soldiers. They were discussing options and had decided that the best course of action was to move on through the southern end of Belgium and cross through it into France as soon as they could, but it would be very cold and hard to navigate through. There were mountains all over the place, and they didn't have a lot of equipment or food.

A short time later, Sergeant Mitchell went up to the other men and provided them with a briefing. After he finished telling them the plan, he told them that they were going to rest until midnight and then they were moving out on a night patrol over the mountain to the other side, where they'd continue onwards with a bearing that took them into Belgium. Once the warning order was complete, the soldiers went to work on their kit as they did their best to get themselves back into a better state.

On April 8, many miles away at the bottom of the ocean off of the German coastline, the British submarine known as the *Sea Dog* was still waiting for the U-boats to leave the area. It had been an unnerving time for all hands, as they could do nothing about their situation but wait.

Corporal Mills snapped his fingers to get the commander's attention when he suddenly heard something very big moving out to sea from an area where there had been no sound activity until only a moment ago. "Sir! I have a really big U-boat coming towards us from the German coastline. It wasn't on my sonar a few moments ago. It appeared out of nowhere, sir," he said with excitement.

Surprised, Commander Biggs walked over to the sonar station and asked for a report. "What exactly are you hearing, Corporal? It better not be a bloody whale again!"

Corporal Mills shook his head but didn't say anything because he was focused on trying to identify the sounds that he was hearing. "It's not a whale, sir, and if it were, it would have to be bigger than a blue whale. This thing is almost two of them put together. Besides its length, though, sir, this thing has some very powerful engines," the corporal said politely.

The commander stood still and then motioned for Mills to give him his headset so he could have a listen. A few moments later, Biggs was listening to a sound that he had never heard before. He listened attentively for several long seconds and then gave the headset back to the corporal. "Thank you, Corporal. Keep monitoring the situation."

Biggs then walked back towards the XO and looked him straight in the eye. "You have the con. I have to go and speak with our guest. Do not so much as lift a tool until that thing is long gone. Pass the order down to all stations right away. Nobody moves. The only thing they're allowed to do is breathe, Lieutenant. I'll be back shortly," said the commanding officer.

"Aye, sir," said the executive officer. Hicks then looked at Chief Petty Officer Rutledge, who had just come on shift, and told him to go and tell every station to stand down and not move an inch for the next fifteen minutes. An unknown enemy vessel approaching their position was his reasoning, he told the chief. Rutledge then left the area and went to make sure everyone understood what was happening at every station in the sub.

A few minutes later, there was a knock on the door to the officer's quarters that Major Babcock had been assigned to stay in. He was inside and working on a letter to his wife when he heard the knock. "Come in, please," he said. A moment later, the door opened and in walked the captain. "Commander, what can I do for you?" he asked as he put down his letter and focused on his guest.

The commanding officer looked at what the SOE agent was doing and smiled back at him. "Major Babcock, you've had the unfortunate experience of having to stay on the sea floor with myself and the rest of the crew as three German U-boats circled the waters making sure the *Neptune* had been sunk. We've been down here now for quite a while, and we even missed our rendezvous with the ground forces we were sent in to support. Do you acknowledge that to be a true account of the events over the last few days, sir?"

The major nodded. "I would say that's an accurate description, Commander—yes. Where is this conversation going? I want to help if I can..."

Commander Biggs scratched his beard and took a moment to think how to best ask him for information. Then, he got right to the point. "I know the reason why those U-boats were protecting these waters, Major. They've got a base somewhere around here, and the biggest U-boat that we've ever heard of has just come out of it and is heading towards our position right now. There's no way we can move one inch until it's long gone. This thing is massive. It's a cargo-size U-boat. I didn't know that the Nazis had U-boats like that. I want to ask you directly what you're hiding from me and from my crew. That's why you're here on this vessel, isn't it?"

Major Babcock was stunned by the news. "I don't know what you mean, Commander. I didn't know anything about a giant U-boat. We're here to support a mission that believed in the possibility of an underground base, but that was inland quite a ways. I had no idea there would be tunnels that connected out to the sea. Is that what you're suggesting we have here?"

Biggs nodded. "That's exactly what I'm suggesting, Major, and the proof is heading right towards us. It's heading out to sea for an unknown destination," he replied.

Major Babcock stood up and walked over to a washbasin. He put his hands into it, bent down, and rinsed his face because he was feeling sweaty and grimy. He knew he stunk, but showers weren't available. He finished splashing water on his face and reached for his face towel and then dried his face with it. He felt better, but the news was making his mind race at a million miles an hour.

"Commander, I had no idea that's what we'd find, but the bombing raids have had their desired effect. The badger has finally come out of its den, and we now know where it lives. We need to get this information back to London at the soonest possible moment. I'm going to assume that the Special Forces can take care of themselves, and we should head back to England at the soonest possible moment. Is that alright with you?"

The commander took a moment and then nodded. "I agree. We need to get this information back to England, and doing so by Morse code is going to give our location away to the wolfpack. We'll head out tomorrow after giving this giant thing time to pass over us and go on its way. Maybe then the U-boats in these waters will disappear and we can get out in one piece. Thank you, Major. Try not to make any noise for the next few hours, though, please," he said as he left the major's room and walked out the door.

At 0830 the next morning, back on British soil, several officers from a Lancaster bomber were set to have a debriefing from an intelligence officer from HQ after their successful bombing raid over Germany. Captain Jonathan Roberts, Lieutenant Rick Peterson, and Lieutenant Frederick King, were getting a debriefing in a Quonset hut on an air force base just out of

Sheffield. As Major Pearce listened, he was stunned to hear their accounts of what had happened on the second bombing mission over the secret underground base in Germany's coastal mountain range near the Belgian border because they were so similar to the accounts of other officers that he had already interviewed.

At first, he thought they were having a bit of fun with him, but after he was assured by the captain that this had indeed happened, Major Pearce gave them each a notepad and asked them to write down the events that had taken place on their mission over Germany.

"How much time do we have, Major Pearce? There are a lot of things I need to write down here," explained the senior pilot.

The base intelligence officer pulled out his package of cigarettes and stood up from his chair. He paced around for a few seconds and then headed for the door. It was a sunny morning, and he wanted to feel the rays of the sun hitting his face. "I'll give you an hour to write down your statements. I'm going to be outside for a bit. You can talk to each other, but don't be talking to anyone else until I send you on your way," Pearce ordered as he reached the exit door.

A few seconds later, he was gone, leaving the navigator and the two pilots to discuss the events that had unfolded on the night in question. Pandora's box was now open for all of them, and after seeing so many of their friends taken out by those balls of light, they wanted to talk about what had taken down so many bombers. There was no question that the so-called 'foo fighters' had been working for the Germans, but they couldn't say whether or not they were manned or not.

Peterson looked at his commander as he twirled the pen in his hands. "What are you going to say, sir? If we tell the truth, it might end our careers," the lieutenant said cautiously. The captain sat back in his chair and thought about that for a few seconds. Then, he let out a big sigh and said, "We lost a lot of planes to those things, Peterson. If we don't figure out what they are, the Germans could take control of the skies all over the world. I don't know if there have been any reports of them in other countries yet, so maybe if we put down the honest truth, it will help the experts figure out what they are, and maybe they can either defeat them or engineer them so we can have them too. I honestly don't know what else to say, but I think he knows about them already from the other crews' statements," replied the senior pilot.

King then picked up a pen and started writing out the date of his statement on the notepad. "Fuck it then. I'm going to tell them what I saw."

Chapter 11

At thirteen hundred hours on April 7, Vera Atkins was escorted into Ian Levington's office downstairs at the Baker Street building. She had been impressed with the décor and walked in with a smile as Mr Levington greeted her cordially. Standing up, he smiled and said, "Vera, I have some news."

This got Ms Atkins quite excited because nobody had heard any updates for quite some time regarding the bombing runs over the German underground base. She sat down in a chair that was on the other side of his desk and then replied graciously, "That's the first bit of good news I've heard all morning, Mr Levington. What are you going to tell me?"

Ian waited for a moment until the door was shut behind the secretary as she left the office. Then he spoke candidly. "We've received word from one of our submarines. Apparently, the second bombing mission had its desired effect and it flushed something out. Something we didn't expect at all."

Curious as ever, Vera wanted to know what he was on about and asked him to come to the point of it all before she had a heart attack from the stress of waiting.

"The *HMS Seadog* is a British submarine, and they were supposed to rendezvous with the 5th SAS Group we sent in and the Royal Marine commandos who were supporting them somewhere near the Netherlands' coastline. Well, that didn't happen because one of the other submarines that were working with the *Seadog* got torpedoed, and all lives were lost, I'm afraid. But then a U-boat wolfpack kept searching and searching the area for any signs that they might have faked being hit. They had a reason for staying there so long, and the Seadog was forced to sit on the ocean floor and wait until they left the area. But they didn't leave. Instead, they protected it. Take a guess as to why they did that?"

Vera answered. "They were trying to protect something? That's my first guess."

Ian nodded his head. "Exactly. They were protecting a secret underwater entrance that went all the way to the underground base. That base in the mountains was a secret U-boat base!"

Vera was shocked. "You're joking? That far inland? How is that possible? We're talking such a great distance to get there from the coastline," she replied as she adjusted herself in the chair that she was sitting in.

"I've no idea, but there's more. While the *Seadog* was on the bottom, an enormous cargo-carrying capacity type of U-boat came out of the tunnel and went straight over their position. They got a really good description of the size. It's longer than anything we know of. What I'm surmising from this report is that this thing is taking cargo out to sea to an unknown location. They could be carrying anything, and now that they know we're onto them, I'm willing to wager that they'll make other U-boat bases in occupied countries that they control. That's why I asked you to come down here. I wanted to check to see how you're going with your plan for the insertion of more agents into France."

Vera wasn't prepared to give him a formal briefing, but she had a good handling of the agents she'd chosen. "I've got them training right now on one of our estates. I only have enough women for three circuits, though. That's twelve women that I need to make the plan work," she replied.

Ian understood that the training process was time-consuming. He stood up and walked over to a map of Europe and pointed to the coastline of Belgium and also of France. "I need your people that you insert into France to be on the lookout for any information about U-boats and secret bases. If the Nazis are moving things by U-boat, they could be building bases close to Germany, France, Belgium, perhaps even Poland . . . I can't say for certain where they'd do that, so we need our agents to be on the lookout."

Vera nodded. "I'll make sure they're briefed about this, Mr Levington. I expect I'll be putting them into France in the coming weeks, but they need support from the resistance and the Special Forces that you've just created. The 5th SAS Regiment as I understand. They were created to support our missions as well as the missions in Belgium. Have you any word about the men you sent into Germany who were from that unit?"

Ian turned around and gave a reassuring smile to Vera. We haven't had word from them as of yet, but that doesn't mean they're dead. They had orders to go into Belgium or France to meet up with resistance forces if they were unable to make the extraction that was planned near the coastline of the Netherlands, and unfortunately, the *Seadog* was unable to get there in time to see if they were there. But don't worry, Vera. We only sent in eight SAS soldiers on that mission accompanied by a platoon of Royal Marines. We have more soldiers training right now to fill the ranks of the Special Forces that we'll need. Many of them are volunteers who have already been fighting against the Germans in Belgium. We'll get their numbers up soon and they'll be able to support your missions as well as missions that are done elsewhere close by. I'll keep you updated, but please continue with your preparations to insert more agents into France. Have you heard anything from the white mouse?" he asked as he sat back down in his chair.

Vera shook her head. "I haven't heard anything as yet. I'll come and tell you as soon as I receive any word, though. So you have no problems with me turning up the volume when it comes to getting my agents selected, trained, and dropped into France then? I'd like to continue on that while you work on building up some support for me to use."

Ian Levington nodded and smiled back at her. "You have my complete support on that, Vera. I'll work on building up the 5th SAS Regiment and finding out where these German U-boats are going. You focus on operations in France, and please let me know if you hear anything about secret bases or U-boat movement around the coastlines," he asked.

Vera stood up and walked towards the door, happy that she had the full support of the British office of the S.O.E. as she thanked him for this urgent meeting. "I'll continue working on things, Mr Levington, and I wish you great success in everything your office is doing. Good luck with it all," she said as she waved a hand at him and then left his office, closing the door behind her.

In the early evening, around 1700 hours, Vera was being driven through the beautiful British countryside in an unmarked vehicle. Her driver knew the area well, as he'd been to the parachute training ground many times before. It was situated on an estate owned by the Tudor family. Alfred Tudor had been a World War 1 veteran who had made a small fortune after World War I had ended by opening up a metal fabrication factory. He wanted to help rebuild the country, and after he had died of natural causes, his family was approached by the Ministry of Defence and asked if missions operated by the SOE could be used to train their special agents for clandestine operations.

"Where would you like me to wait for you, ma'am? SOE Agent Kent asked as he pulled up near where the female agents were situated in the early evening hours.

"Just wait for me by the mansion, and I'll make my way over to you as soon as I've finished," she said. One of the training instructors saw her vehicle and walked towards it while several other instructors continued their work in a giant barn that had been modified for learning how to do static parachute drops.

"Good evening, Ms Atkins. My name is Agent Denison. I'm the senior parachute instructor here. If you'll come with me, I can take you into the barn to see how the training is going.

Vera smiled and replied, "That would be lovely, Agent Denison. Thank you. How's the training coming along?"

Denison smiled back at Vera as they walked towards the extra-large barn and the sun began to set. From inside, they could both hear some yelling. Somebody had stuffed up and was getting a verbal reprimand. Within a minute, Vera could see the tower that had been built inside it. That was where the candidates would climb up and jump off. A second or two later, the harness that they wore would engage and it would seem to them like they had just shuffled out the door of a plane and performed a static jump. Upon landing on the ground, they would roll and then recover their parachute.

One of the women who had just done her jump from the tower had failed to look up towards where her canopy would have been in a real jump, and she was being scolded for not checking. Vera didn't interfere because, in practice, the instructors were there to catch and correct the mistakes before they became real. When they were being dropped into the unknown at night, there would be no one to catch their errors before they made a fatal mistake, which might see them die as a result.

The female candidate didn't talk back. Instead, she realized her error and joined the line again to do the jump a second time. They had been at this all day, and it appeared like they wouldn't be stopping until the instructors were satisfied with their progress. As Vera watched them, the female agents saw her talking to the senior instructor off in a corner as they observed the training. Each of the women took a glimpse at her and wondered who she was but then focused on the task at hand when one of the instructors started shouting orders. He spoke to make the point register. "If you ladies jump out of a plane and want to live, I'd advise you to remember that you're going to be hitting the dirt hard, and if you don't know where it is, you'll break something, and I guarantee you that if the Nazis find you, you'll be shot for being a suspected spy. Remember that once you're out of the plane, you count to three and then look up. One, two, three . . . check canopy! Say it!"

The candidates then repeated in unison, "One, two, three . . . check canopy!"

"Very good. Again! Say it!" yelled the instructor as he paced around the ground, looking towards the twelve candidates.

The ladies kept doing their drills but shouted out loud, "One, two, three... check canopy!"

At eight o'clock that evening, Vera entered a guest room at the Tudor estate and took her suitcase to the bed, where she placed it. There were only enough items in there for one night. She wanted to stay on the grounds and watch the women she'd selected to see if there were any cracks in their psychological profiles.

After putting things in the bathroom and then in the top drawer of a dresser near the bed, she walked over to her jacket that she had been wearing all day. She pulled out a cigarette from a packet that she had placed in one of the outside pockets and walked over to the door that opened up to the balcony. There was a beautiful view from where she was, but the sun was setting, which made the gardens look quite spectacular. She decided to take a moment for herself and contemplate how much longer she would have to wait before she could schedule the missions to insert the three teams of four into occupied France.

After she was done with her cigarette, she would go downstairs to meet with the senior instructor to talk to him about her agents and to see if they could get all the training that they needed in such a short amount of time. The calmness of the night on the estate was a bit shocking to her at first. She was alone with her thoughts, and she thought about a number of things as she stood on the balcony. She wondered what was going to become of the agents that were now in training.

At sunrise on April 10, Corporal Babcock was looking at Corporal Tanner's toes on his right foot. Though it was spring, Mother Nature had brought them snow and some very low temperatures overnight as they rested on the side of another mountain, but now they were on the Belgium side. Not moving for the previous six hours had caused one of Tanner's toes to discolour, which was concerning.

"Can you wiggle your toes?"

Tanner tried to wiggle them, but he couldn't feel anything as Carl touched the underside of his purple middle toe with a stick. He tried it on the underside of his foot too, and there was no pulling away. "You're starting to get frost bite, mate. We need to warm up your feet somehow. Maybe we could get behind some rocks and start a small fire to boil up some water? Then use the steam to warm up your toes? What do you think of that idea?" Corporal Babcock asked as Sergeant Mitchell came up to see what the verdict was.

After looking at Corporal Tanner's frostbitten foot, Sergeant Mitchell realized he would also need a clean pair of socks, so he went back to his rucksack and pulled out a pair of woollen ones for him. He brought them to the injured soldier who was working on finding dry bits of wood from underneath a fallen tree.

"Don't make a huge fire. I don't want to see a lot of smoke. If we get seen, I'll be bloody pissed off. So boil some water and then put the fire out as quickly as you can. After you've dried your foot, put on these dry socks and put your other ones over top of them. Are all your socks wet?" The sergeant asked as he looked down at Tanner.

"No, Sergeant. I've used them all, but I think one pair is still dry. I'll put those over the ones you're giving me. Thank you," the corporal replied as he accepted the clean pair of socks from him.

Sergeant Mitchell continued checking on the other soldiers to see if anyone else was injured from the cold of the night. There was snow all over the weapons, and that worried everybody. As he went from soldier to soldier he saw Lieutenant Colonel Plante looking at a topographical map, but he left him alone and continued doing a foot inspection.

As Corporal Babcock looked at the small fire that was starting to show flames, he was also worried about creating too much smoke. He put more fist-size rocks around it and started putting more feather sticks over the flames. They were dry sticks, so he was hoping they would produce more flame than smoke. For the moment, it seemed like they were out of danger. Now all they had to do was find the resistance forces that were known to be in the area approximately fifty miles away from where they presently were. To get over the remaining mountains would be an impossible task with the snow all around them. In his opinion, they needed to get to the train tracks that littered the countryside and follow them carefully until they were closer to the area that they needed to reach.

A short time later, the patrol moved on, heading over the vast countryside, which was quite rocky and hard to traverse. There were bits of snow to be seen on the higher ground that they were heading towards, but they weren't moving in a straight line. Sergeant Mitchell was being strategic, doing his best to make it hard for them to be seen by using the ground to their advantage. The downside to this was that it was going to take a lot of effort and a lot of time.

Later that afternoon, Corporal Oliver came up from behind the patrol. He'd been put at the rear of the group and had the task of watching their rear arc in case anyone snuck up on them. He called out for Sergeant Mitchell, and the patrol stopped to let him catch up and speak with the sergeant.

Corporal Babcock wondered what was happening, and from his vantage point as the point man, he could see that their platoon commander wanted to know what Oliver had to say too. A few moments later, Sergeant Mitchell and Corporal Oliver met and knelt down on one knee as they discussed something important, but Carl had no idea what they were talking about because he was too far away and the wind was starting to blow a lot of the dry snow in his face, making it hard to see.

He returned his gaze to the front and decided to move forward some more to see what was down in the valley below them. When he reached a nearby tree, he pulled out his binos and took a look through them. What he saw shocked him. There was a plane down there, and it was a big one. Now he had news to share with the platoon commander also.

Meanwhile, Corporal Oliver informed Sergeant Mitchell that he had spotted a Nazi patrol that was following their trail with dogs. They were at least three miles away, but they had their scent. The SAS commander showed up and asked what was happening and was shocked to hear the news. "How many did you see, Corporal?" the patrol commander asked as he looked behind him and saw Corporal Babcock coming towards them.

Oliver didn't mince his words. "I saw at least fifteen soldiers and three dogs, sir. But they're not even at the base of the mountain yet, so they'll have a hard time climbing it when it's getting close to dark," he answered. Sergeant Mitchell took out his binoculars and looked at Corporal Oliver. "Which way did you come from? I want to see this for myself," growled the sergeant.

The SAS corporal pointed in the direction that he had just come from, and Sergeant Mitchell picked up his sub machine gun and said, "Okay, you join the front of the patrol, and I'll take Tanner with me and put him as our rear guard. Tanner, come with me," the sergeant ordered just as Corporal Babcock arrived on the scene.

Plante looked over at him as he quietly approached and knelt down next to Oliver and the commanding officer. "Sir, I've got news. I've caught sight of a British bomber that's crashed down in the valley ahead of us. I don't see any smoke and a lot of it is covered in snow, but there are bits of metal that are shining in the sun," he explained.

The SAS commander was shocked. "What? Maybe that patrol isn't after us at all. It could be that an enemy fighter patrol shot it down and reported it and now they've sent out a hunter force to find the crew. Shit. This is not a good situation for us to be in since we have all this information we need to get back to England. We've got to avoid going down there. Find us another route, Corporal. Can we climb higher and make it harder for the hunter force to find us? Go and see if you can find us a new route out of here, Babcock. We still have loads of mountains around us. I know there's a train track around here somewhere. I'll pull out my map and have a look at it while I wait for Sergeant Mitchell to return.

A moment later, Corporal Babcock went back to the front and started looking for a new way to get them to their next objective just as Sergeant Mitchell was observing the Nazi soldiers who were trying to reach the base of the mountain in a lot of snow. He looked down the mountain through a haze of fog that had decided to stay near their present altitude. Mitchell stopped looking through his binoculars and pointed down at the base of the mountain. "Look down there," he said to Corporal Tanner. "You'll see at least fifteen Nazis that are on our tail."

Corporal Tanner looked through his own binoculars in the direction that his sergeant was telling him to study closely. "They might not be after us. Babcock's just told the C.O. that there's a Lancaster down in the next valley. It could be a hunter force that's been dispatched to find the crew," Tanner suggested to the sergeant.

Sergeant Mitchell was amazed to hear that bit of news. "Holy shit. Well, when it rains it pours, doesn't it? We shouldn't be going anywhere near that plane," he said.

Corporal Tanner put down his binoculars for a moment to looked at Sergeant Mitchell. "I heard Plante say that he wants to find another route now. He's looking for train tracks while Babcock is looking for another route over the mountains so we stay away from the British bomber. You're wanted back there right away. I'll watch these guys, but I don't think they'll make it through all that snow before it gets dark, and it's going to get really cold tonight. You can tell," the corporal replied.

Sergeant Mitchell looked down at the corporal's injured foot. "How are the toes? You might be right about it staying below zero up here overnight. You'd best be taking care of that foot because we can't have any fires to thaw it out this time around," he said firmly.

Corporal Tanner nodded. "It's fine, Sergeant. That extra pair of wool socks is keeping it warm enough, and I have a feeling in my toes again thankfully. It's going to be dark in a few hours, though. I guess we'd better continue on through the night and try and put as much distance between us and them as we can," said the highly trained soldier.

Sergeant Mitchell agreed with the corporal's assessment. "Okay then. If they get closer to us, let us know. I'll make sure we don't lose you, but keep looking out for the man in front of you. I want us to keep moving, and I'm willing to wager that the commanding officer is going to want to do that too," he replied as a cold wind hit his face. Then, he put his binoculars in their case, and with his weapon on his shoulder, he went back to join Lieutenant Colonel Plante as he left Corporal Tanner to watch the rear arc. That night was hard for everybody. The eleven men were pushed to the extreme, but they continued onwards over several mountains. They did their best to make their journey challenging and brutally hard so that if the Nazi's were in fact after them, they would have one hell of a time trying to catch them.

Just before sunrise, however, Lance Corporal Potter smelled wood smoke and stopped everyone. They were in the middle of nowhere, and they were starting to go down into another valley. They didn't want to walk into a camp hidden in the treeline that was full of sleeping Germans so they were extremely cautious and sent a small team down to find out who was down there being so careless. They sent one man who was still dressed up as a German soldier and one of the men who was wearing a British combat uniform who just happened to be Corporal Babcock.

The two took their time and descended the side of the mountain quietly. There was a 900-yard descent before they reached the tree line, so by the time they got there, a lot of light was coming down from the sky, making their job a bit easier. As they looked around, they saw no sentries, no signs of a big camp with camouflage netting, no artillery emplacements or tents. The only thing that they could hone in on was the campfire. Somebody was just trying to stay warm.

When Lieutenant Jeffries woke up from the boot he'd just felt kick his ass, he rose with a fright and saw a man in a British combat uniform and smudge marks all across his face. There was a submachine gun staring at him too. After he got his breath back, he reached over and touched the shoulder of the man sleeping beside him. They'd been sleeping with their backs to each other on a bed of spruce branches to keep themselves off the ground. When the other fellow rolled over, he too got the fright of his life when Corporal Babcock gave him a cheery smile and said, "Good morning, sleeping beauties."

The other soldier went for his sidearm, but Carl quickly jumped over Jeffries and pointed his SMG right at his chest. "You fire that gun, mate, and I guarantee you a bullet in the brain. Just stop what you're doing. I'm with Special Forces. Just relax, mate. I'm not here to hurt you. So don't worry. Okay? We good?" Carl asked as he gave the man a few seconds to think things through.

Eventually, the shivering co-pilot nodded and stayed still, which allowed Carl to move away from both of them so they could see him. "What are you fellas doing way out here in the wilderness? Are you from that bomber that my group saw back there? What're your names?"

"My name's Jeffries. Lieutenant. Daniel Jeffries. I was the co-pilot on that plane. This is my rear gunner, Corporal Morgan. We're the only ones that made it. The others are dead."

Babcock was saddened by their story. "Well we were the ground forces on that mission, and because of you, my team got underground so we owe you a debt of gratitude, mate, but guess what? That campfire led us right to you. We could smell it from way up there, and my partner and I have been sent down here to find out who was sleeping in these woods. Now have you eaten anything or had any water in the past few days?"

Corporal Morgan shook his head. We were doing good with rations. We only ran out of them a few days ago," he replied, but we've both got frostnip in our toes and fingers I think."

Carl looked at them both. They looked dehydrated. "Okay, first thing we're going to do is I'm going to share my canteen with you guys, and then I'm going to give you the food that I have on me. Share what I have between you two, and then we'll be off. Just so you know, though, my partner is hiding behind that tree up there and he's dressed like a Nazi, so whatever you do, don't be stupid and shoot him, okay? We had to dress up as Germans to get down inside the underground base. Are you okay with me calling him out?"

The lieutenant nodded as he took Babcock's canteen. "Okay, call him."

Carl looked behind him and called out to his sidekick. "Hey, mate. It's okay. They know that you're behind me. It's safe to come out now," the corporal said. A moment later, a man dressed as a Nazi soldier came out from behind the tree. It shocked both the Lieutenant and the gunner. "Jesus Christ! You weren't joking were you?"

Corporal Babcock shook his head. "You don't have to worry. If we had been the enemy you would already be tied up. Let's put snow on that fire right now, and you can eat my rations. Once we have something in ya and take a look at your hands and feet, then we can get back up into the high country. We know there's a hunter force out there because we've seen them. We think they're out looking for the crew to that Lancaster. So, the best option for you two is to join our group and come along for the ride I reckon."

Lieutenant Jeffries handed the canteen over to Corporal Morgan and then asked Carl, "Where are you guys headed?" A moment later, he looked down at the boots that he was wearing and started untying the right boot so Babcock could take a look at his feet before they set off.

As the man dressed up in Nazi clothing walked up to them, he answered the question. "We don't know yet, but we plan on getting as far away from your plane as humanly possible. I have some rations too, so you can each have something to fill your guts with," he said in a friendly tone.

After giving these two men their extra socks, they set off hiking uphill. It was hard on Carl's lungs, but that's why he'd volunteered to go and find out who was in the woods beneath them. He wanted to see if he could get his lungs working properly and test his balance as he walked down to the alpine forest.

Lieutenant Jeffries noticed that Carl was having a difficult time of it. He observed that Carl was sweating and breathing quite hard. "You sound like you're not feeling very well, mate. Are you sick with the flu?" he asked.

Babcock turned and looked at Jeffries. He shook his head. "Nah, mate. I was in the woods when your bombs blew us all up. The concussion blasts from those things lifted me right off the ground. They seemed like they were the most powerful explosions that I've ever experienced in my life, and I've been through the wringer, let me tell ya!"

The lieutenant was shocked to hear that some of the bombs that they'd dropped had exploded on friendlies. "Oh my God. Was anyone else hurt? Those weren't your everyday bombs, Corporal. There were three bombs that were connected to each other. Each one of them weighed in at four thousand pounds of explosives, so twelve thousand pounds went off near where you were?"

"I'm not sure. It happened at night. We couldn't see the bombs coming down but we could hear them just before they connected with the ground. There were quite a few explosions around us, and trees were flying everywhere. We were in the woods taking out the anti-aircraft guns that were hidden under nets. It's hard for me to talk and walk uphill at the same time, mate. I'm trying to catch my breath. Let's stop for a second," said the corporal as he raised his arms above his head a few times to allow a few full lungfuls of air to be breathed in and exhaled. Then, he returned his arms to his after a minute or so.

"There was crazy cloud cover that night, and I'm sure some of your bombers were dropping their payloads off target. The bombs that landed near us helped take out some of the anti-aircraft emplacements, but unfortunately, two of our men were killed. Sergeant Mitchell found me alive but unconscious and dragged my sorry ass out of the woods. I'm forever in his debt. So, the two of us didn't go underground with the others. They were long gone by the time we came out of the forest. We made it to the ORV, though, and waited for them. Eventually, they showed up, and we set off to head into Belgium. Then, we found you. I'm testing my lungs right now, and by the looks of things, I'm still not back to full working order," Babcock explained. "That's where we're at."

The Lieutenant was shocked by the story but wanted to know more. "What did they find underground? We hit that position twice. Was it worth it?" he asked softly as birds started chirping nearby.

Corporal Reece then added, "We lost everyone on our plane but us two. We've got skin in the game too, Corporal," he said sadly.

Lance Corporal Drummond, who was dressed up at the Nazi looked over at Jeffries and Morgan. Then he nodded and gave his response to the question. "We lost half of our men down there. Our platoon commander was killed, and many of my friends got killed as we tried to get out of there, but yes, we got answers, though we're not allowed to reveal what we saw. You can ask the Patrol Commander who you'll be seeing when we re-join the main group up on the top of that mountain. I'm sure you'll be amazed by what he tells you. I'd suggest that we continue, though. You lads ready?"

Carl nodded. "He's right. You'd best ask Plante about what we saw. We lost a lot of good people, but hopefully, we'll be able to get that information back to British Intelligence and something good will come of it," he said as he stepped off and resumed hiking uphill over the rocky terrain.

By thirteen hundred hours, Babcock's group had reached the top of the mountain and it was quite cold with clouds taking over the sky above them. The two airmen were taken to see Lieutenant Colonel Plante, and they were given a debriefing. Corporal Morgan and Lieutenant Jeffries had many questions about what had been seen underground. The SAS commander didn't want to talk too much about it, though. All he would tell them was that it went deeper than they'd thought and that the Germans had been using slave labour to build the facilities beneath the mountain. Every time the patrol commander thought about what his men had been through, it caused him emotional pain.

"Lieutenant, I'm sorry for the loss of your crew on that bomber. Without your bombing mission, we would never have gotten ourselves down there. There is a burden on us now to get the information that we have back to England as soon as possible, which is why we're going to move in a different direction than the coastline. My belief is that the hunter force is actually after you, and it would make sense to them if you headed towards the coastline as an avenue for escape, but what we're going to do is to meet up with the resistance, and hopefully, they'll be able to assist us further, getting the information we recovered back to England."

Jeffries realized he had no say and stayed silent, but Corporal Morgan still had some questions. "Sir, we're not dressed for this cold weather. How long do you think we'll last out here? We're not commandos like you guys are. We're from bomber command. We have to report something just as important as whatever it is you discovered underground. If you were on the ground that night, did any of you see the balls of light that were causing our planes to crash into each other? The Nazis have some kind of super weapon that can fly at impossible angles and at great speed. We all saw dozens of them coming at us that night. We need to get back to England and report this; otherwise, when we send more missions into Germany; we're going to lose more men and more aircraft. Shouldn't that be of concern as well?"

Plante was angered by the corporal's tone but realized he wasn't well trained for the mental stresses caused by situations such as the one they were in. He looked from Morgan to the sky and said, "There was cloud cover that night, so we couldn't make out much on that second bombing raid, but we've seen those balls of light on the first mission that your bombers did. I agree with you that this is of real concern, and I have every intention of sending you back to England so you can report what you saw. Right now, though, you're going to become members of my patrol group, and we're going to work together to survive this. What we'll be doing over the next few days is moving on foot towards the railways, and I'm hoping that eventually, we're going to meet up with members of the resistance forces that I know personally. They're out here, but we have to find them. Now can I ask if either of you have any weapons or ammunition on you?"

Lieutenant Saunders was the first to reply. "Yes, sir. We each have a pistol with three clips but nothing more than that, I'm afraid," he replied.

Plante shook his head. "A lesson for next time if you ever go up in the air again, Lieutenant. Always have a Plan B in case your initial plan fails on you. Each of you should have had a daypack, at the very least, with essentials to help you with escape and evasion, but because you don't, my men now have to lend you their kit as a consequence of you not being prepared. And they might never get their stuff back if you get killed. Even if it's just a pair of socks, out here, we only have what we brought with us. On top of the kit, though, there are other things that you have to have that are just as important as the items you pack with you. I'm talking about emotional resilience and then having a strong body to carry you the distance. Together, they'll help you solve the problems that you'll face out here. Is that clear?"

Corporal Morgan nodded his head before Saunders did because he knew he'd upset the SAS commander. "Yes, sir. It's a huge lesson for me. You're right, sir. I'll know better for next time . . . if there is a next time."

"Yes, sir," replied the lieutenant. "We should have been better prepared than we were. We didn't pack much because we didn't want to jinx ourselves and get shot down."

"And how did that work out for you in the end, eh?" the lieutenant colonel asked sarcastically. Plante then asked the two men how they were physically and was curious about their cold injuries.

They both replied that they were cold and couldn't warm themselves up.

"I have a solution for you. Sergeant Mitchell, can you get me those extra uniforms, please? I think I have a use for them now." As soon as the Patrol Commander made the request, he saw Mitchell start reaching into his rucksack, and a few seconds later, he pulled out a German officer's complete field uniform. Then, Corporal Tanner went into his rucksack and pulled out another one and brought it over to the sergeant.

"Thanks, Tanner," he replied as he took it from the corporal and brought both of the uniforms to Jeffries and Morgan.

"You want us to dress up as Nazis, sir?" the lieutenant asked quite shocked as he looked at the uniforms.

Plante stood up and adjusted his wool cap with his right hand. Lieutenant Jeffries surveyed the SAS officer who was now standing in front of him and found that he looked quite strong. "That's right, Lieutenant. One thing about the Germans is they make a good kit for their soldiers. That jacket and those pants are made out of wool. They'll warm you up, and since you don't have very much clothing on you, I wouldn't complain about it. What I would suggest, though, is that when we reach the train tracks, the two of you keep a low profile so the resistance doesn't shoot you before they see the rest of us! They'll have snipers with them, and they are very good shots. They hate Nazi's and with good reason. Do you have any more questions that you want to ask me before I give the order to move out?"

"No, sir. Thank you for helping us get out of here. We'll wear the uniforms and keep a low profile. I guess we'll stay at the rear of the patrol?"

Lieutenant Colonel Plante then nodded his head and looked over at Sergeant Mitchell as a sudden gust of wind blew in his face and the rain started to announce itself. "Sergeant, let's get going in five minutes. We need to get moving. Put these two at the back of the patrol, but have somebody behind them to make sure we don't lose them as we move along."

The sergeant did up his rucksack, and while he was doing it, he knelt down on one knee and said, "No problem, sir. Lieutenant Jeffries, if you and Corporal Morgan would come with me when I'm done here, I'll put you at the rear of the patrol," said the sergeant.

Then, the eleven men checked their gear, and a few minutes later, they set off again, hoping that if the Nazis were pursuing them, they would have great difficulty doing so because of the routes that they'd been making for themselves thus far.

Chapter 12

On the afternoon of April 11, in the coastal area of the Netherlands known as Zeeland, Captain Kurt Sommer was unloading fresh fish that he and his first mate, Derek Lang, had just brought in on his moderate size commercial fishing boat. Lang was down in the hold filling a large cargo net full of their catch, which had nearly been filled to capacity. On the main deck, however, Sommer was distracted as he observed several Nazi soldiers escorting a man dressed in civilian clothing as they walked towards another fishing boat at the local marina. Kurt tried not to look conspicuous as he observed what they were doing, but he watched attentively through the corners of his eyes as they boarded the vessel and poked around as if they were looking for something.

Kurt walked over to the open hatch and looked down at Derek before he spoke to him softly. Just to make sure he wasn't heard, he decided to bend over as if he was yelling orders at the deck hand below. "Derek, there are two Nazi soldiers and some sort of official on the pier. They're boarding another boat in the same marina as us. They're checking papers and inspecting his boat. Is the radio hidden away so they won't find it?"

The first mate stopped working and looked up at the captain. "It's not here. I took it off the boat in pieces two nights ago while the engineer was working on your engine. There's nothing on the vessel that would give us away. As far as they're concerned, they'll only find fish aboard!"

The news was quite reassuring, and a broad smile took over Sommer's face as he nodded and stood back up. Suddenly, he heard the captain of the boat that was being inspected yell back at the German official, and moments later, the German soldiers grabbed him and forced him down flat on the deck of his boat.

Kurt moved back to the hatch and looked at the cargo net that was full of several kinds of fish. "They've just arrested the captain of that boat. I know him too. He's not the type to go and do stupid things, so somebody must have tipped the German's off about something he was doing," he said as he looked away from the event taking place on the pier.

Derek put the last big fish onto the cargo net. "That's not good. They'll inspect every boat in this marina after that and want us to divulge everything we know about him. I'd suggest we go back out to sea as soon as we can," said the first mate as he signalled that Sommer needed to get behind the controls and lift the cargo net out of the hold.

It was only a few hours later when a different German official saw Kurt out on the pier moving his catch from his boat to the fish factory on a dolly one barrel at a time. The man identified himself as Peter Wagner, and he told him that he was an inspector of some kind. Wagner asked the captain of the *Blue Gem* to answer some questions to which he replied that he would, but he explained that the fish would spoil if it took too long. Mr Wagner saw the many barrels of fish back at the boat waiting to be moved and understood the captain's position.

After fifteen minutes of questions, while standing still on the pier, the inspector was satisfied that Kurt Sommer was telling him the truth. This wasn't his homeport, the inspector discovered, and he was just delivering a load of fish to the local factory before refuelling and setting off back out to the open sea. Still, the eye contact and the types of questions were very hard to navigate, and when it was over, the inspector asked if he could interview the crew but was advised by the captain that his crew had left for the day and would be returning the next morning. Then, they would be leaving the harbour. Wanting to know where his crew had gone, Kurt replied that his first mate had gone to a whorehouse to get laid since they'd been away from home for quite some time. That made the inspector smile, and he left, satisfied that Kurt posed no risk to the occupied country. Kurt watched the inspector as he looked at another boat suspiciously while walking away.

An hour after sunrise the next morning, Captain Sommer and his first mate were at sea and quite happy to be out of that port town. They'd made enough money to refuel the boat and have some money in their pockets, but they were still worried. The German Navy was constantly patrolling the coastline of the Netherlands, and it was in their best interests not to stick around in any one place for too long. Kurt looked out the main window as he steered his boat out to sea. His engine seemed to be working really well.

The door to the wheelhouse suddenly opened, and Derek stepped inside. "Oh, it's windy out there. It might mean another storm front is coming our way," Lang commented as he looked into the eyes of his boss.

Sommer looked at the compass and steered the boat towards Belgium. "We're leaving these waters, Derek. That was too close for me," he said to his friend.

The first mate understood where he was coming from. He looked behind the door and saw the portable chair that had been placed there. Derek grabbed and unfolded it, then sat down. "The engine's running much better now, I'd say. I'm glad you had a marine engineer come and do a rebuild before we headed out. It must have cost you a small fortune to rebuild that small engine," Lang said.

Captain Sommer looked at Derek and nodded his head and then grunted. "It was time to do it. I've been taking my chances for too darn long on that engine as it was. We could have died out in that storm off of the German coast. I made a promise to God that if he got us out of it, I would rebuild that engine, and I'm a man of my word," Kurt said.

Derek looked at the steering wheel and the compass from where he was sitting. He could see the direction that his captain was taking them. "We'll soon see how this old girl works. This morning, I kept thinking that the inspector you mentioned might show up any minute," replied the first mate.

The captain kept watching out the main window of the wheelhouse, and then a few moments later, he accelerated the engine so that it was performing at maximum capacity as he watched the clouds on the horizon come towards them. As the boat moved through the ocean at a faster clip, he looked back at Derek and said, "well there's only one way to find out. Let's test it out for a while and see if it can handle some speed. What's the story with the radio?" Kurt asked.

Derek looked over at the barf bucket that was resting a few feet from where he sat. He was pleased to see that it had been cleaned and emptied. He looked at the coat rack behind him a second later, checking to ensure that they had their raincoats hung up there in case they were needed at a moment's notice. When he saw that they were there, he turned back to his captain and said, "I didn't bring it on board at all. I hid it on the shoreline quite a ways from here in an old boathouse near the cabin that I once lived in. I used to play throughout the entire forest of the local area with my brother when my father worked at the cannery," he explained.

"How far away is it? We'll have to wait until high tide to get closer to shore," said Kurt as he listened to the engine perform at full throttle.

Derek pondered about the distance as he looked out the main window from where he was sitting. He could still see a fair amount of blue sky, but the clouds would soon take it over. "I think it's about an hour from where we are now . . . about ten to fifteen miles at the most."

The captain was surprised by how far away it was. "How on earth did you make it there and back in such a short time span?" Kurt asked as he looked down at the map that he had put in front of the steering wheel to confirm the bearing the boat was on.

"I got a ride back to a lady friend's house that lives out that way. I told you I would be seeing her. We go back a long way," Derek replied, almost blushing.

Captain Sommer looked straight at him and asked a direct question. "Did she see the radio? Was she suspicious after you left her home?"

Lang shook his head and said, "I took the radio out of this boat in pieces in my bag. She never knew that I had it on me. She was happy to see me again and wanted me to move back to that town, but I don't think I could do it. I didn't divulge anything. I listened to what she's had to live through. She was raped by a Nazi officer, so I don't think she's on their side," said the first mate as he looked down at the wooden floor of the wheelhouse.

Still, the liaison was a worry to Kurt. He spoke his mind almost immediately as he thought about what he wanted to say to his first mate. "The Nazis use fear to get people to reveal things about other people, Derek. You should know this. If she was raped once they could have threatened to rape her again unless she turned somebody in when she had a lead. You didn't see that boat captain arrested. I did. That Inspector Wagner fellow didn't question you; he questioned me about everything under the sun. We must be careful. We'll be shot if they find out what we do with that radio. We're spies for the British, remember? We'll go and get it. Then, we must leave these waters for a while. Perhaps we should consider going over to England? What do you think of that idea?" asked the captain as he turned the wheel and steered the boat onto a new heading.

As the *Blue Gem* moved through the water at high speed, they observed another commercial fishing vessel heading out to sea. There would be more boats venturing out from their ports as the fishing fleet went out to work on the open sea.

Derek looked at his captain and said, "I think it might be something to consider. Perhaps we should send a message back to England and see if they'll consider allowing us to go over there if things get too hot for us to handle where we are? Who knows what they'll say in response," he said, wondering whether or not his former girlfriend would rat him out and throw him to the wolves. He stood back up and said, "I'm going to go downstairs and see how things look. The engine sounds okay, though. Would you like me to make us some coffee?"

The captain stayed at the wheel and steered the boat. He turned and looked at his first mate and gave him a friendly look. "Yes, after you check the engine again. See if there's any oil leaking from it. It sounds pretty good, so hopefully, everything is alright down there," he said before returning his gaze to the birds that were flying out in front of the vessel.

Lang opened the door and walked out onto the main deck. He shut the door behind him and walked along the metal floor as he headed back to the side door that led down to the galley, the cabins, and the engine room. He was still lost in thought about his former girlfriend and didn't pay much attention to the dark clouds that were looming off in the distance.

By six in the evening, the weather had started to get a bit rougher and the sun had set. The captain had made the decision not to go closer to shore until after dark so as to have the cover of darkness working in their favour. As he peered out the side door, he looked to see how Derek was doing getting the skiff into the water and to determine if his help was required.

What he saw pleased him. The small boat was already in the water and he was lowering the oars into it. In a few minutes, his first mate would be on his way, and with some luck, they wouldn't be staying around for much longer than the two-hour maximum he'd told his first mate to stick to for a schedule.

With the anchor lowered, Kurt Sommer turned off the engine and left the wheelhouse. He went out of the wheelhouse and headed to the rear of the boat where the side door was located. He needed to eat, and this was the opportunity to make himself something that he would enjoy. As he got to the stairs that went down into the bowels of the boat, he took a moment to make sure that Derek was on his way by giving him one last look before he went down inside his ship.

He listened and could hear the oars smacking the water. Derek wasn't so great at using them, but he'd get the job done soon enough. High above the fishing boat, a gull baulked at the intrusion that the boat had made on his fishing grounds, but then he landed on the top of the wheelhouse and thought that it was a lovely perch where he could take a rest and observe the choppy sea. Off on the horizon, the skies were pink and colourful from the setting sun, and the wind was picking up. These were sure signs that a storm was brewing, so that helped the captain decide to just have some soup in case he had to vomit it all back up later in the night.

In the mountainous area between Belgium and France, Lieutenant Colonel Plante and his Special Forces group were heading south-east as they continued along the train tracks that they had discovered several days before. It was April 13, and to their surprise, they hadn't found any resistance forces sabotaging the railway lines that they had been travelling on as they had hoped. The senior officer wondered if they were working on operations further into France as he watched Sergeant Mitchell and Corporal Babcock lead the patrol forwards over the snow-covered tracks under the light of a full moon.

Being short on supplies, things had grown increasingly dicey. It was getting colder as they stuck to the mountains. The French Alps weren't very far away from where they were—perhaps another three days of walking. Switzerland wasn't very far away either. Both afforded them opportunities, but if they chose to go to the Swiss side of the equation, they might be held there indefinitely until the war ended, and the commanding officer was only getting started with his new SAS unit, so he wanted to avoid that option if it were at all possible. This is what he decided as he took in the breathtaking view.

It was getting dark, and they had talked about jumping on a train and catching a ride, but there was always the chance that the Germans would have an armoured guard on the train they jumped on, and if they lost their opportunity to get back the information that they had accumulated since April 1, then all the lives that had been lost would have been for nought. These thoughts plagued his mind until, finally, he stopped the patrol and had a one-on-one discussion with Sergeant Mitchell.

While the other soldiers watched their arcs of fire for signs of enemy movement, the patrol commander and Mitchell walked away from the men so they could talk without being heard. When Plante felt safe enough, he opened up and told his second in command what he was thinking. "Sergeant, I'm worried. We should have run into somebody from the resistance by now. I think we need to self-rescue. We're out of food, and we're wearing all of our clothes that we packed with us. I think we need to leave these tracks and head into the valleys below and hunt for something. At this point, I don't care what it is, but we need to feed ourselves or we're going to lessen our chances of succeeding on this mission. Do you think there's any sort of animal down there in the forests below that we could shoot with our silenced weapons? Maybe a deer or a wolf?"

Sergeant Mitchell looked down the side of the mountain. It was a steep descent, and they'd probably get killed if they went down the side of the mountain that they were on. He tried to come up with another option when suddenly, Lance Corporal Potter, who was taking his turn at the rear of the patrol, yelled out that there was a train coming towards them.

Plante swore several times in frustration. They were out in the open, and there was no tree cover. Plus, they had no winter whites to hide themselves in the snow. The cliffs above them were steep and covered in ice and snow. They couldn't be guaranteed solid footholds as they worked their way up. The only option was to hide below the train over the side of the mountain. The C.O. walked over to the side of the mountain and suddenly realized that it was almost suicidal to go down it, but they had no choice. They could hear the train approaching. He looked at his men and gave the order. "Over the side and hold on for dear life. Don't go farther down than you have to. Just hide and don't get seen! Let's go!"

Quickly, the men obeyed the order, but once they saw how dangerous this was, they started thinking of ways to do it without getting killed. Lance Corporal Smith spotted a trellis only a hundred yards away. It wasn't a big one, but several of them ran for it anyways while others stayed and climbed down below the tracks. Those who stayed behind went over the side and managed to find good footholds and soon were praying to God that they would live to see another day as the train rode past them one by one, which caused the rock to vibrate and shake as it went by.

As Babcock tried to keep himself firmly in place below the tracks against the side of the mountain, he had difficulties holding himself in place with and all of his equipment that he was carrying because of his missing finger—the one that he'd lost in Papua New Guinea. He did his best to find footings to hold his weight up with his legs, but he couldn't hold onto everything, and as a result, he lost hold of his weapon, which had slipped off of his shoulder and slid down his arm on the sling. He tried to keep it, but it was just too awkward, and when he lost suddenly lost one of his foot placements, he had to move his hands to get a better grip on something else to prevent himself from falling. In absolute horror he watched his rifle fall down to the bottom of the mountain hitting rocks along the way and no doubt rendering it inoperable.

Above him, the sounds made from the train cars were very loud. Corporal Babcock cringed as he heard the metal wheels grind on the tracks above him. It seemed like there were an endless number of train cars attached to the engines, but after nine minutes, the train had moved over them all.

Corporal Babcock had managed to survive another ordeal that he would have to write his father about. As he waited for somebody to give the all-clear, he continued to hold on for dear life as the cold winds blew around everyone, making their fingers quite cold. *What would the old man say?* he wondered. Once the train had disappeared, Plante gave the word to climb back up onto the tracks. To his delight, nobody had died, but two other men had also lost their rifles, so he knew that the heat for doing so would be shared. The commanding officer knew that they hadn't been able to hold onto their weapons under the given circumstances and unfortunately they'd lost them.

Soon, they caught up with the soldiers that had made it to the trellis and had hidden safely underneath it. When Sergeant Mitchell saw Corporal Tanner, he asked him to pull out the German pistols that they'd taken off of the dead German officers that they'd killed. As soon as the corporal handed them over, Mitchell took them and gave them to the men who had lost their rifles. "At least you have something you can shoot back with. Now let's get the fuck off this mountain and head down and see if we can recover those weapons you guys lost. Maybe we can fix them. Then we need to find us some food and some shelter. Let's look for a route down," the sergeant said to everyone as they heard the train continue on its journey.

The next morning, Ian Levington, the intelligence officer for the British section of the Special Operations Executive, was escorted into Maurice Buckmaster's office, where he and Vera were waiting anxiously for this urgent meeting that had been scheduled by their secretaries. As he walked into Maurice's office, he greeted both Vera and her superior with a respectful smile. "Good morning. How is everyone?" he asked pleasantly.

Maurice responded by standing up and extending his hand. Ian shook it and then heard Maurice's response. "I'm well, thank you, Ian. Thanks for coming in to see us so early in the day," he said curiously.

Vera greeted Mr Levington back with a smile and asked, "What news do you have for us today about your missing Special Forces group? Have you heard from them yet?"

Ian sat down and was offered a cup of tea by Maurice, which he declined politely because he'd just had one not half an hour ago downstairs after his debriefing with Major Babcock. "No. There's no news from them yet, but I just saw one of our new agents who was on the HMS Seadog—the submarine that confirmed that the Germans have a giant U-boat transporting goods and equipment to unknown parts of the world. He had quite the story to share with me," he replied as he looked in Vera's direction.

Vera responded almost immediately. "Major Babcock was, as I understand, to be assigned to F-Section, was he not? He never got here. Your British section assigned him to a submarine? Why weren't we told about this, Mr Levington? I thought we shared information between our offices?"

Levington paused for a moment as Maurice gave Vera a stern look and then said, "Easy, Vera. Let's hear him out shall we?"

Ian looked at them both and said, "And that's what I'm trying to do now if you'll let me finish, Vera," he scolded. "We were short on manpower that could speak the French language, and we thought that we should have agents in every submarine who dropped off Special Forces or who might need to pick them up or perhaps even members of the resistance groups that are operating all around these areas. We had to be ready for an emergency extraction somewhere down the line. We lost one of our agents on the Neptune. He was also supposed to be going to F-Section. I'm sorry about that, and I'll find you replacements," Ian said to the two of them.

Vera's eyebrows rose. "What do you mean, *replacements*? Aren't we getting Major Babcock now that your submarine has returned?" she asked with uncertainty.

Ian Levington looked her directly in the eyes and shook his head. "There's more news. We know that the Germans have been working on a number of secret projects including balls of light, which have crashed our bombers into each other, and giant U-boats. We also know that Hitler is sending people all over the world right now to find things. Rumour has it that he even has the Spear of Destiny in his possession."

Maurice looked puzzled. "What's the Spear of Destiny, Mr Levington?" Maurice asked, looking a bit puzzled.

Mr Levington looked in his direction and replied, "It was the spearhead that killed Jesus Christ Maurice. Whoever has possession of it is rumoured to be unstoppable, and that has emboldened Hitler and the Third Reich. So, back to Major Babcock: the short answer to your question, Vera, is no; I still need him. We're short on submarines, and we're sending the message out fast to our Navy to be on the lookout for unusual U-boat activity with orders to sink any U-boats that come into their sight and of course to report observations of them too. As it happens, there are rumours that the Germans are sending teams into India and Tibet. Major Babcock just came from that area before he joined the Special Operations Executive, so I want to send him back there on a different mission. I can't reveal much more than that at this time, but if you'll allow me to have Major Babcock for a time, I'll return him to F-Section when he's finished, and in the meantime, I'll find you some new agents to make up for the ones that I've stolen from you. I realize you have concerns about supporting the agents you're about to drop into France," he said, which caught Vera's attention straight away.

"You're right. I'm weeks away from dropping my agents into France Mr Levington. As far as I can tell, we only have a few isolated pockets of resistance forces there right now to help us. If you want Major Babcock for your mission, then I'd ask for you to help me by inserting more Special Forces into France and Belgium, but to make matters more complex, the existing resistance groups that are there need more supply drops. Will you give me the manpower and the planes to do so?" Vera asked in a strong tone.

Ian smiled. "I've not come empty-handed, Vera. You'll have the planes that you need and the supplies to fill them within a week, and yes, the 5th SAS regiment has almost got thirty new members added to its ranks, as I understand, from new recruiting and training cycles in Northern Scotland. I just checked on those numbers yesterday. We can prep them for a new mission and insert them into France and Belgium, and hopefully, those countries will start building up their resistance to the Third Reich. Are we agreeable to these arrangements?" he asked as he looked back at Maurice and then back to Vera's glance. There was silence for a few moments.

Maurice broke the ice by saying, "If you deliver what you're saying you'll bring to the table, then yes, we have a deal. Good luck hunting down those German U-boats, and if I might add, don't forget that France has a coastline too; I'm sure there's plenty of German U-boats travelling along it. The Netherlands too since it's all occupied by the Nazis," he said from behind his desk.

Levington smiled. As he received a cup of tea from Buckmaster's secretary he looked over to Vera and said, "you're right about that, Maurice. I have to put more eyes out there to watch for U-boat activity. Vera, if you could get your resistance forces that we put in there as well as your new agents to watch out for U-boat activity in your area, that would be appreciated, and I'll start putting more eyes and ears out on the islands throughout the Pacific," he concluded.

Vera got the last word in as she stood up to help the secretary bring in the tea trolley a bit closer to them all. She looked over at Mr Levington and replied, "I'll do the best I can with the support that you give me, but I wish you every bit of luck in hunting down those dreaded U-boats. They're causing havoc out in the Atlantic shipping lanes, but now that they have come out with bigger versions, that's a real worry to us all, isn't it?" she said as she handed a cup of tea to Maurice.

"It is, indeed. We'll get on it right away. Thanks for your understanding and letting me use the major on the mission to India. I promise that I'll make it up to you," Levington said as he smiled at them both and sipped from his cup. A minute later, the secretary left the room and closed the door. As soon as she was gone, they resumed talking about their plans for France and how their spy networks should be set up.

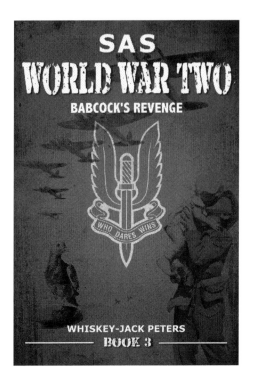

While Hitler's U-boats continue to move supplies and people all over the world, the Special Operations Executive is scrambling to set up observation posts on uninhabited islands in the Pacific. There is a shortage of manpower, and because Germans technology is so advanced, the allies are worried that their communications might be overheard. New plans are put into action that could help, but will they be able to stop the Nazis from developing their superweapons that British Intelligence believes are being developed? What has become of the SAS team that has made it into France? Will their information get back to London in time? The war rages on...

Manufactured by Amazon.ca
Bolton, ON